ALSO BY LAURENCE YEP

Sweetwater

Dragonwings
A 1976 Newbery Honor Book

Child of the Owl

The Serpent's Children

Mountain Light

The Rainbow People

Tongues of Jade

Dragon's Gate
A 1994 Newbery Honor Book

Thief of Hearts

The Dragon Prince

The Imp That Ate My Homework

CHINATOWN MYSTERIES

The Case of the Goblin Pearls
Chinatown Mystery #1

The Case of the Lion Dance
Chinatown Mystery #2

DRAGON OF THE LOST SEA FANTASIES

Dragon of the Lost Sea

Dragon Steel

Dragon Cauldron

Dragon War

EDITED BY LAURENCE YEP

American Dragons
Twenty-Five Asian American Voices

LAURENCE YEP

The Case of the

FIRECRACKERS

CHINATOWN

Mystery
#3

HARPERCOLLINS PUBLISHERS

Library of Congress Cataloging-in-Publication Data
Yep, Laurence.
    The case of the firecrackers / Laurence Yep.
        p.   cm. — (Chinatown mystery ; #3)
    Summary: When a prop gun used during the making of a television show
turns out to have real bullets, twelve-year-old Lily Lew and Auntie, her
movie actress great-aunt, comb San Francisco's Chinatown in search of the
culprit responsible for loading the gun.
    ISBN 0-06-024449-6. — ISBN 0-06-024452-6 (lib. bdg.)
    [1. Mystery and detective stories.   2. Chinese Americans—Fiction.
3. Chinatown (San Francisco, Calif.)—Fiction.]   I. Title.   II. Series: Yep,
Laurence.   Chinatown ; 3.
PZ7.Y44Cag   1999   98-55056
[Fic]—dc21   CIP
                                                                                        AC

Typography by Al Cetta   3 4 5 6 7 8 9 10   ❖   First Edition

TO MY AUNTIE JO, WHO WAS THE KINDEST,
MOST GENEROUS SOUL EXCEPT WHEN SHE PLAYED
MAH JONG. THEN SHE SHOWED NO MERCY.

—L.Y.

CHAPTER ONE

'd had a lot of practice at stakeouts, so I tried to look inconspicuous. Lounging against the wall, I pretended to casually read a comic book. Every now and then I glanced over the top of it at the door, waiting for the perp . . . I mean, victim . . . no, target . . . no, subject.

At 8:03 A.M., the door opened. Ten seconds later, the subject emerged in her best clothes and high heels.

Auntie stopped dead in her tracks and stared. "You're in a dress. Who died?"

I tried not to blush. "There's no funeral. Can't I put on something nice when I feel like it?"

Auntie felt my forehead. "Ah, I can feel the hormones beginning to rage. Take two aspirin and go to sleep for ten years."

I hooked my arm around Auntie's, determined not to let go. "I thought we were partners."

"Remind me of that the next time a bill comes in," Auntie cracked. She'd been famous for that in her Tiger Lil movies. She pressed a fingertip against my nose. "You were listening to me yesterday on the other line, weren't you?"

I kept my death grip. "In our profession, we prefer to call it surveillance." After helping Auntie with two cases, I thought I'd better do research, so I'd been watching a lot of cop shows.

Mostly Auntie was an actor, and a good one with a long string of credits in Hollywood. Recently, though, she hadn't been getting too many nibbles, so she'd shifted her base to up here in San Francisco—though she still took an acting job when it was offered to her.

In the meantime, she'd set up a public relations business; and then, because she kept meeting unemployed actors for whom she felt sorry, she had started finding them jobs, so she'd also become an agent.

On top of everything else, Auntie never saw a mess that she didn't have to tidy up, so she'd done some detecting as well. Auntie Tiger Lil had enough energy for a dozen people.

Auntie rolled her eyes. "Oh, for the good old days when you only wanted to watch cartoons." Then she looked at me. "Now all you can think of is Clark."

Clark Tom was the teenage heartthrob of millions on the television show *East Meets West*. And his signature phrase, "Gotcha," had become a catchword across the country.

"That's not true, Auntie. I just don't want to disappoint my friends." I held up the bag of autograph books that my schoolmates had given me.

At first I was afraid that Auntie was going to refuse. That would have left a long line of my friends mad at me.

To my relief, Auntie grinned. "I guess since I don't pay you, I owe you a few perks. Come on, kiddo."

As we passed the kitchen, Mom poked her head out of the doorway. "Don't you want some coffee, Auntie?"

"No time," Auntie said. "I've got an appointment."

Mom placed a hand over her heart in mock surprise. "Oh, really?" She hadn't gotten any of the family's acting talent. "I don't suppose . . ."

Auntie motioned to me with a sigh. "Give the auto-graph books to Lily."

Mom passed me a bag as big as mine.

"Mom," I scolded, "you weren't supposed to tell anyone."

"Oh, autographs?" Dad said, popping up behind Mom. "Is it anybody famous?" He was an even worse ham than Mom.

Auntie cut to the chase. "Give the books to Lily."

Fortunately, Dad had only a couple, so I didn't have to rent a U-Haul.

When we got outside, though, we found my big brother, Chris, waiting uncomfortably on the sidewalk. He didn't have a stack of autograph books. What he had was a lot worse: his latest girlfriend.

Instead of standing in his usual slouch, Chris was standing up straight. Instead of wearing his usual baggy clothes, he was dressed to kill. "Auntie, I want you to meet my classmate, Evie Li."

Evie was all fizzy, like a soda bottle that someone had shaken up. "I'm so pleased to meet you. Chris has told me all about you. I'm so thrilled."

"Really?" Auntie asked, glancing surprisedly at Chris. He dropped his eyes, shuffling his feet sheepishly.

My big brother had always been pretty awful, but he'd gotten to be a real pill ever since he started going to high school three years ago. I wasn't against all his causes. In fact, some of them were pretty good ones. It was just the way he went about promoting them. He had to get in your face and badger you.

Among other bits of badgering, Chris had made clear what he thought of Auntie's career. He thought she had sold out to the Hollywood producers. While he had never been rude to Auntie's face, he'd also never bothered to hide his contempt. So it was strange to have him bragging about her.

As Evie got more excited, she chewed her gum faster, so I caught a faint whiff of Juicy Fruit. "I haven't been able to see any of your movies," she confessed, "but I was hoping to meet you. I'd like to ask your advice about acting."

Auntie was still cautious. "Really?"

Evie seemed like the complete opposite of the serious girls whom Chris usually hung out with. I didn't see what they had in common at all. She must have hypnotized him.

I nudged Auntie. "You can talk later. We've got a business appointment."

"Oh," Evie said in a disappointed voice.

Chris blocked our way. "I was hoping we could come along with you to meet . . ." It took an effort to bite out the words. "Clark Tom." He'd also made it clear what he thought of Clark's show, *East Meets West*.

4

"I didn't tell him," I swore to Auntie. In fact, lately I had avoided Chris because he always wanted to lecture me on something. "It must have been Mom who blabbed."

Auntie pinched the bridge of her nose. "Make a note, Lily. 'Get own private line.'" She lowered her hand. "One that no one else can listen to," she said pointedly.

Evie pressed the tips of her index fingers together. "Chris said you wouldn't mind."

I could see the muscles working on my brother's face. He hated to beg to see someone he despised, but he also wanted to make Evie happy. "Please, Auntie."

Auntie glanced back and forth between Chris and the girl. It was obvious my big brother was eager to impress Evie.

Auntie was a softy at heart. "Sure; why not, kiddo?"

It was a typical San Francisco morning in August—foggy. The damp air brushed my face like a wet washcloth as we walked down the hill to Chinatown. I always loved that view in any weather, but the fog made the tiled, curving roofs seem like they were floating in the air.

However, when we got to the edge of Chinatown, we saw how Hollywood had transformed it. One of the main streets through Chinatown had been blocked off, and police were standing around, redirecting traffic and keeping back the crowd that had gathered. All around, curious faces watched from the apartments overhead. Since it was Saturday, when a lot of people came from other areas into Chinatown to shop, the other streets were really going to be a mess later.

"Look at the idiots," Chris murmured to me. My

brother hadn't lost his scorn for television.

"I think it's neat," Evie declared.

I waited for Chris to bore us with his list of the flaws in the show, but all my big brother said was "Okay."

My jaw almost dropped open. Evie was able to do something that not even my parents could do: get Chris to shut up.

The street itself was filled with big trailers and an army of snakelike cables wriggling all over. Lights stood like giant sentries around a camera that was set up in front of the laundry. I felt like I was seeing an invasion from outer space.

Chris got on his usual soapbox. "Look at all the energy they're wasting."

"Now, Chris," Evie said, taking his arm. "Behave."

And wonder of wonders, he clammed up.

I couldn't decide which was stranger: a silent Chris or a machine that spewed out mist like someone smoking a giant cigar, even though it was already a foggy day.

"What's that machine?" I asked Auntie.

"A fog machine. Apparently San Francisco isn't foggy enough for them." Auntie chuckled as we came to the barricade.

One of the police officers turned when he saw it was Auntie. It was Officer Quan, whom we'd met on Auntie's first case. A string of priceless pearls known as the Goblin Pearls had been stolen, and Auntie and I had tracked down the thieves. I'd helped her on that case and the next, in which I'd helped her track down a bomber who had hurt a lion dancer.

"Come to catch the thieves in the act, Miss Leung?" Officer Quan asked.

"There won't be any thefts with you on duty," Auntie said.

Officer Quan looked sour. "I'm going to try my best."

"Oh, sure," Auntie said uncertainly. "Um, we've got an appointment."

Heads began to swivel so people could stare at her, and I heard hurried whispers.

"If you say so." Officer Quan dragged the barricade to the side so we could slip through the gap. "Good luck. You might need it."

There were about a hundred people on the street eating from little cardboard boxes.

Evie pointed at them. "Why are they out here? Did some restaurant close?"

"Some of them are crew, and some of them are probably extras," Auntie explained. "Film companies bring in a caterer to feed everybody."

Auntie asked one woman where Clark was. The woman bit into an apple from her box breakfast. "Last time I saw him, he was with Carl, the prop guy, in the prop room, in that little trailer over there." She waved the apple vaguely toward the trailer.

A man standing nearby lowered his cup. "I just left him in the courthouse with his fellow gods." He pointed toward a tiny shack.

"I never heard of a courthouse in Chinatown," I said to Auntie.

"Neither have I," Auntie admitted. "The old Hall of

Justice used to be east of Portsmouth Square, but that area wasn't part of Chinatown then."

The "courthouse" was awfully small. In fact, it was just a shack attached to a laundry. The owner must have been pretty desperate, because there were all sorts of things in the laundry window—everything from stuffed dolls and postcards for sale to a sign advertising a five-cent copy machine.

Outside the courthouse, some of the film crew were setting up ladders. Packets of firecrackers were heaped in a small hill next to them.

"That's more firecrackers than you used to open up the Fishers' restaurant," I said to Auntie. And I had thought that was a lot.

On the front of the courthouse I saw a sign announcing that the Judge of the Dead was inside. As we got near the dark doorway, I hesitated. For some reason, the place gave me the creeps—as if there were something inside waiting to grab me.

"This is so thrilling," Evie bubbled. She took out another stick of Juicy Fruit and popped it into her mouth without taking out the old gum. At that rate, by the end of the day, she'd have a wad the size of a softball in her mouth.

As she eagerly walked toward the shrine, she threw down the foil and yellow wrapper. "Hey, don't litter," I scolded her, and I picked it up.

Chris would usually have lectured anyone who wasn't careful about the environment, but he just trailed behind her like some placid cow.

I stared. "What's gotten into him?"

"It's love, kiddo." Auntie chuckled.

"If that's love, I never want it." I frowned.

Evie was the first through the doorway. Suddenly she gave a shriek and ran outside, into Chris' arms. And when Chris peered past her, he yelled too.

Auntie had trouble running on her high heels, so I passed her quickly.

When I first saw the monsters glaring at me from inside, I nearly jumped out of my skin.

Seated on a throne was a huge scowling man. He was surrounded by creatures that had human bodies but the heads of oxen and horses. Incense sticks had been stuck into a bowl of sand in front of him.

Auntie squinted. "That looks like one of my old boyfriends. Now what was his name?"

"Sinners, step forward and be judged," a voice boomed from behind the statue. "But be afraid, very afraid, for the Judge of the Dead knows all your sins."

I grabbed hold of Auntie. "Yikes!"

Auntie patted me on the shoulder. "Since when did the Judge of the Dead speak English?"

At that moment, Clark Tom stepped out from behind the throne. "Since he got me to do his voice-overs." He tapped one knee of the stern judge.

I almost jumped when the statue's head began to nod. Clark snatched his hand back almost immediately.

Crouching carefully, he checked the lower half of the throne. "One of the legs looks wobbly. I'll get Props to fix that."

"Where'd you get him?" Auntie asked.

Clark rose again, chuckling. "A regular terror, isn't he? He was part of an old wax museum in Chinatown before it shut down. My producer, Manny, found him gathering dust in a warehouse. We needed a shrine for the episode, so Manny dug him out again."

Clark stretched his free hand into the darkness. He must have done it to flick a switch, because small spotlights illuminated various parts of the room. Everywhere, there were statues of people being tortured by the ox- and horse-headed creatures.

Some of the things there made my skin crawl, and I turned away.

"This is worse than that horror movie I saw last week," Evie said.

Chris suddenly looked jealous. "Well, it wasn't with me."

"It's about the same as shooting two weeks in a jungle with an ape that could outact the guy playing Tarzan," Auntie said.

She had made a lot of movies in her career, just about all kinds. Some of them had been in weird locations.

Auntie put her hands on my shoulders. "We've got a twelve-year-old here. Kill the spots," she said.

"Sorry," Clark said. "The research people tell me that in the old days, each temple in China had a room just like this. It taught the young and old what happened to sinners. Different tortures for different sins."

"She'll learn about that soon enough," Auntie snapped. "Now kill the spots."

The lights went off, except for the one on the Judge of the Dead and his servants. "When it's your time, the Judge of the Dead sends his servants to fetch you." Clark dusted one of the horse-headed statues with his hand. "It is said that long ago an ancient king and his army were about to be defeated on the battlefield by his bitterest enemies. He prayed to heaven for a final victory, and heaven granted his wish. But he and his entire army were sent to the Yellow Springs to judge the dead. No sin goes unpunished."

"You've really gotten into the mythology," Auntie said.

Clark rubbed his stomach. "Yeah, well, I've had some stomach trouble, so all I could do was read in the hotel. I think that darn caterer gave me food poisoning."

Spitting out her gum, Evie whizzed past me. "Clark, I'm your biggest fan."

I thought Clark was going to give her the brush-off, but he just stared at her. "Turn your chin."

Puzzled, Evie started to move her head.

"Wait," Clark said, and Evie froze. He took a step back and moved around, studying her from different angles. "You've got quite a profile."

Evie squirmed excitedly, and then remembered to hold her pose. "Really?"

Chris shoved forward with a scowl as big as the Judge's. "He's just playing a joke, Evie."

Clark didn't pay any more attention to Chris than if he had been a fly. "Evie? Is that your name? Have you done any acting?"

"Not since my freshman year," Evie said, afraid to turn her head.

11

"Just how old are you?" Clark asked.

"Seventeen," she said. She was smiling as if she thought this was better than an autograph.

"Stick around, will you?" Clark said.

"Now just wait a moment," Chris protested.

"I don't belong to you," Evie snapped at my brother.

"Let's not get excited," Clark said, trying to soothe them both.

"It's bad enough what your lousy show does to people's minds, but I won't stand for this," Chris said, pulling back a fist.

If Chris had paused to ask me, I could have warned him that Clark not only studied kung fu but did a lot of his own stunts. That included most of his own fight scenes. One moment Chris was lunging toward Clark, and the next he was flat on his back.

Angrily, Chris tried to scramble to his feet, but Auntie plopped down on him like a wrestler. "Whoa, there, tiger. You're outmatched."

Evie hovered over Clark. "Are you hurt?"

"Naw," Clark said with an easy grin. Not even his hair was mussed.

"What about you?" I asked Chris.

"Just his pride," Auntie said, studying Chris from her perch on top of him.

Chris was lying there, looking embarrassed. "I don't know what got into me. You don't solve anything by violence."

"I'll get security," Clark said, heading for the door.

"That won't be necessary," Auntie said, nodding her

head at her human seat cushion. "Clark, I'd like you to meet my nephew, Chris." She motioned toward Evie. "That's his friend, Evie Li."

Clark took me by the hand. I think a good percentage of the women in America would have melted at that touch. I'm afraid to say that my knees got a little weak. "And you're . . . Lily, right?"

I was shocked. "You . . . you remember me?"

"How could I forget?" Clark chuckled. "You were rolling along the street, dressed up like a jar of Lion Salve and demolishing a parade, until I stopped you."

That had bugged me ever since. Because I didn't want any of my friends to know I had worn such a clunky costume, I'd never been able to tell anyone that I had been rescued by Clark Tom.

"I was chasing after a thief, and I tripped," I said, blushing.

I suddenly remembered all the autograph books, but before I could mention them, Clark nodded at Auntie. "Say, whatever happened to the pearls?"

"The pearls were actually stolen by the owners," Auntie said. "It turned out to be an insurance scam."

Clark raised an eyebrow. "That might make a good episode," he said thoughtfully.

Chris tapped Auntie on the back. "Hey, remember me?"

"I haven't forgotten you, kiddo," Auntie said.

Chris slapped the ground like some struggling wrestler. "I give up, Auntie. It's past the ten-second count."

Auntie squinted one eye at him. "Are you going to behave?"

"I'll see to it," Evie said, taking his hand. "You bad boy."

Auntie held up a hand, and I helped haul her to her feet. "Oof. You should've stuck to your diet," I whispered.

"Remember? I decided not to be an ingenue anymore. I'm a character actor now," Auntie said in a low voice.

"Tiger Lil, you still got the zip, the zing"—Clark snapped his fingers rhythmically—"the snap, crackle, pop, and that's what the show needs."

"You want Auntie's cereal?" I asked, puzzled.

Fortunately, Auntie could translate Hollywood talk for me. "You want me to write some dialogue?"

"More than that," Clark said eagerly. "The show's finally going to give my character the main story line for a bunch of episodes."

"Warren must have blown his stack," Auntie said. Warren Grey was the star of the show, and Clark was his sidekick.

"Warren's got his eye on a film career," Clark said, "so he's finagling time to do movies. That's how I got this episode built around me. Warren's off in Tunisia."

"This is your chance," Auntie said, sizing up the possibilities.

Clark spread his hands. "Everyone—from the sponsors and network on down—thinks it's time I got involved with someone." He lifted his head. "My people think there could be an Emmy for me at the end of the season."

Having hung around Auntie enough, I knew that an Emmy was an award for television actors.

I pointed to Auntie and then to Clark. "You mean a

romance between Auntie and you?"

Clark looked a little startled, but he recovered quickly. "Sort of. If your Auntie was . . . um . . . ten years younger, she could play the role."

Auntie dimpled. "I'm not that young, Clark. Make it more like fifteen."

It was Auntie's turn to be scrutinized by Clark. "It's going to be hard, but I bet our makeup people can make you look old enough. They're real artists."

"Old enough?" Auntie asked puzzled.

"You'll be part of my girlfriend's family," Clark said.

Auntie rubbed her chin. "It'd be a stretch for my fans, but I guess they'd accept me playing her mother."

Clark scratched his head. "I think the writers had a grandmother more in mind."

I realized finally that Clark had just been trying to save Auntie's pride.

Auntie started to shake her head. "Well, I don't know. . . ."

Clark really poured it on. "I know it's not quite what we discussed originally, but it would give your fans such pleasure to see you on the screen again."

Auntie winced. "I'm not ancient history, you know."

"I know, but there's a whole new generation of fans waiting to meet you," Clark said.

Auntie eyed him uncomfortably. "I don't know, Clark," she said. "I'm pretty busy."

"We'd make it worth your while," Clark said.

Auntie waved a hand airily. "It's not that I need the money."

I expected Auntie's nose to grow as long as Pinocchio's. Auntie's public relations business paid the bills, but she also insisted on representing local actors. Even if they didn't have more talent than a rock, my softhearted Auntie would sign them up and then have to advance them money. As a result, she was still operating all of her businesses from a desk in my mother's beauty parlor in Chinatown.

"Then do it for the fun," Clark said. "And teach me some of your tricks."

Auntie stared down at her big black bag as if asking its advice. Finally she shrugged. "Well, why not?"

"Great," Clark said, shaking her hand. Then he beamed at Evie. "Stick around. We're casting the role of my girlfriend this week."

If Evie'd had any doubts, she would have lost them under the intensity of that smile. "Do you think I really have a chance? I'm not a professional."

"Neither was I when I started," Clark said, and he nodded to Auntie. "And it's great that you already know Tiger Lil. I can see the chemistry."

Chris suddenly whispered something to Evie. Whirling around, she began arguing with him, also in a whisper. "I'm staying, Chris, and that's final."

"It's just a come-on," Chris insisted. "You'll be sorry," he said.

I was glad when he left the room before he got into any more trouble with Clark.

"Chris," Evie said in distress, but Chris kept on walking.

"He'll get over it, kiddo," Auntie said.

When I heard the shouting outside, I thought it was Chris, getting into more trouble. I hurried toward the door, but Auntie was even quicker.

CHAPTER TWO

When we got outside, we saw an old Chinese man lecturing the film crew.

"You should be ashame!" the old man was scolding them. "You make fun of Lord Yen-Lo." I guessed that was the name of the Judge of the Dead.

"Not him again," Clark muttered. "Funny old geezer. He's been giving us a hard time ever since we started filming."

A couple of members of the crew were tying strings of firecrackers together to make even longer strings. Paper wrappers lay scattered all around.

One of the crew began to climb the ladder with a staple gun in one hand and a long string of firecrackers in the other. "So who cares, Pops?" she said.

The old man kicked at the mound of firecrackers. Brightly colored packets went flying, scattering over the sidewalk. "I not your father."

"Thank heaven," the crewperson said.

"This place fake!" he protested.

18

"It's just television." And she stapled the firecracker string to the front of the courthouse for emphasis. "Your boss was happy enough to get the fee. And we're letting him do all the costumes."

The man tried to yank the firecrackers down. "You make Lord Yen-Lo mad. He make lot trouble. Everyone will be sorry."

At that moment, a gray-haired man in a blue suit zipped out of the laundry and grabbed the troublemaker. "Shut up, you fool. They're paying me a lot of money for that storeroom. I'm not going to lose my fee because of you."

The old Chinese man waved the firecrackers. "But these people bring big trouble to Chinatown."

"I gave you a job here because I felt sorry for you," the man snapped. "If you want to keep it, you'll keep your mouth shut."

"It not right," the old man said, but he let himself be pulled back toward the laundry.

"Thanks, Mr. Li," Clark called to the man in the blue suit. As they disappeared inside, Clark shook his head. "If that old guy hasn't complained about one thing, then it's been another."

Evie had taken a step toward the laundry. "He ignored me."

"The old geezer?" I asked.

"Mr. Li," Evie said.

"Do you know him?" Chris asked.

"That was my uncle," Evie explained. "I haven't seen him since I was small, but I recognize him from his photos."

"Well, maybe he didn't know you. You've grown up," Auntie said.

Evie shook her head sadly. "No. He just looked right through me like I wasn't there. It has to be the feud. He and my father were business partners, but then they had a fight, and he left. When my dad tried to start over, Uncle wouldn't help us out. They haven't talked since."

On Auntie's last case, we'd had to deal with another Chinatown family feud, and I knew how messy they could be. "That must have been some fight."

Evie shrugged. "I don't know much. My parents don't like to talk about it. I've just picked up bits and pieces from what they've said to each other. When I've asked them about it, they just clam up. My father and my uncle have ignored each other since the feud. And I guess that extends to me."

"Why don't you try talking to him now?" Chris suggested.

"Do you think he'd listen?" Evie asked.

"You can save the reunions for later," Clark said impatiently. "I want you to meet my producer, Manny," he said.

"I guess," Evie said shyly.

Poor Chris, I thought. He was going to be trolling the ocean for a new girlfriend pretty soon.

Evie tried to walk beside Clark, but a sullen Chris slipped in between them. She gave him a scowl that would have terrified the Judge.

Clark led us to a trailer where a boxy air conditioner was going full blast—though it was cold outside. There was also a small satellite dish on top. "My home away from home," he said, and he opened the door.

Inside, it was cold enough to be a refrigerator, and every appliance besides the air conditioner seemed to be on. I heard three different televisions as well as a stereo.

A young man sitting in a chair jumped to his feet right away when he saw Clark. "Get you something, Clark?"

"Want some java, Tiger Lil?" Clark asked.

"Sure," Auntie said.

"Tea for me," Evie said.

"A juice," I said.

"Sorry, we're out of juice. Soda okay?" the young man asked.

"What kind of joint are we running, Eddy?" Clark demanded.

I felt sorry for Eddy, so I said, "A soda would be fine." Chris also asked for a soda.

"Right away," Eddy said, bustling around the kitchen.

In the living room, ignoring the televisions and stereo, was a bald man with a beard reading a newspaper called *Variety*.

"Manny, have you met Miss Tiger Lil?" Clark asked.

Manny immediately got to his feet. "I haven't had the pleasure, but I've been looking forward to this." He shook Auntie's hand. "I write and produce this show."

"You wear a lot of hats," Auntie said.

Manny rubbed his head. "That's why I lost my hair."

"This is my great-niece, Lily Lew," Auntie said, introducing me.

Manny shook my hand with just as much enthusiasm. "Ever acted?"

I thought of my one bad experience with the theater. "Nope; Auntie used up all the acting genes in our family."

"That's a shame," Manny said. "The camera would love your skin." Placing a hand beneath my chin, he tilted my head up. "Look at that face, Clark."

Evie wasn't so pleased to be out of the spotlight. "A little makeup would help," she said sweetly.

"Naw, she's perfect as she is," Manny said, moving my head to a different angle. "Great cheekbones. Make wonderful flat planes that love the light."

I think Manny was trying to compliment me, but he was making me feel like a piece of meat. Fortunately, Auntie saw how uncomfortable I was and came to my rescue.

"Evie is really the discovery," she said.

So Clark introduced Evie to Manny. "Wonderful, wonderful," he said mechanically. I wondered how often he and Clark had been through this routine. You could almost see the steam rising from Chris, though.

"I'm glad you're looking for people," Auntie said, setting her bag down on the coffee table with a thump. "I've got some local talent you might not know about." She pulled out a stack of folders.

Manny sighed. "Sorry, Tiger Lil. I've got all the extras I need." He jerked a thumb toward the door. "Didn't you see them outside gobbling down breakfast?"

"But you need fresh faces, and I don't think there was anyone over twenty-five," Auntie said. "You'll forgive me, but there's more to Chinatown than young boys."

"Not in our Chinatown." Manny shrugged.

"Well, I'll leave these with you for future reference." Auntie hunted through the files and then opened one. I saw an eight-by-ten of Norm, a part-time actor I'd met when the Goblin Pearls were stolen. He was also an assistant district attorney. "Now here's a face that just screams law enforcement."

Manny stared at the photograph and shook his head. "He looks like a shoe salesman." He closed the folder. "But I'll pass all these on to the casting agency we use. Thanks."

He should have known that he couldn't put off Auntie that easily. "What's their name and number?" she asked. From her bag, she produced a pen and notebook.

Manny rolled his eyes at Clark, who just shrugged. No one escaped Auntie.

Clark leaned his head close to Evie's. "You hungry?"

"Not really," Evie said.

"How about some eggs?" Clark asked, and without waiting for an answer he turned to the young man who was serving us our drinks. "Eddy, some eggs."

"Gotcha," Eddy said.

Clark frowned. "That's my line, Eddy."

"G— I mean, sure thing," Eddy said, and he rushed toward the kitchen.

"She said she didn't want eggs," Chris said.

"Well, whatever you do, don't eat that poison the caterer's serving," Clark warned.

Manny's tone was conciliatory. "We've been all through that, Clark. This is just nerves talking. The caterer didn't give you food poisoning."

"It was all I ate that day," Clark said. "I got sick as a

dog, but I worked anyway, since I didn't want to hold up shooting. But it'll be a lot worse if everybody else gets sick too."

"It's more likely the beginnings of an ulcer," Manny said. "I ought to know. I've had three of them."

"Well, *I* say it's the caterer." Clark looked around at the rest of us with a raised eyebrow. When no one asked for anything, he said, "Eddy, just one order of eggs."

"Got— I mean, right," Eddy said.

Clark turned to his producer. "Manny, the Judge is a little wobbly."

Manny was preoccupied with a sheaf of papers Auntie had put in front of his face. "Shame on him for drinking this early."

"I think it's the legs to the throne. Better get someone to fix it," Clark said.

Manny turned. "We can't. That's a rental. We're not supposed to change a thing. It's in the contract. The collector is very fussy. Unless you want to buy that thing as a doorstop. Don't worry. You only have to shoot some dialogue scenes in there."

"Well, if I don't lean against it, I guess it'll be okay," Clark said.

I worked up enough nerve to mention the bags of autograph books. "Mr. Tom—"

He flashed that smile at me. "Clark."

"Clark, would you mind signing a few books?" I asked, hauling over the bags.

Clark eyed them unhappily. "That looks more like a library."

24

"He's too big a star," Chris said sarcastically.

That stung Clark. "Only too happy to oblige my fans," he said. "Evie, would you mind helping me?"

Evie practically flew over to Clark. "Sure; what do you want me to do?"

"Open the books for me to a blank page," Clark said.

As he signed, he kept on flirting with Evie, who seemed pleased by all the attention. Chris sat, drinking his soda and getting redder and redder as he glared at the pair.

Auntie was still busy pitching her "kids" to Manny—Auntie called all her acting clients "kids," even the eighty-year-old one—and I kept sipping my soda.

When Clark was done, he brought the books over to me. "There you go. This should keep your friends happy."

I didn't mention that some of those friends were middle-aged.

Unfortunately, Clark noticed my drink right then.

"Eddy," he said in an annoyed voice, "I don't see a lot of bubbles in Lily's soda. It must've gone flat in the can."

"Sorry, Clark," Eddy said, hurriedly opening another can of soda.

"I'm fine," I said.

"No, you got to have bubbles," Clark said. "Hurry up, Eddy."

Eddy scurried over to me. I held up my glass in embarrassment. As Eddy poured more soda into my glass, Clark wriggled the fingers of one hand. "Where's my coffee, Eddy?"

Eddy instantly looked apologetic. "Sorry. I guess I didn't hear you, Clark."

Actually, I don't think Clark had asked.

I tried to think about what it would be like to be a teenager like Clark, with all that power and the money and the fame. I guess it would go to my head too. What had that first crewperson said? Visiting with his fellow gods.

Eddy scurried back with a mug of coffee.

Clark stared at it. "That's not my mug."

Eddy shrugged apologetically. "I couldn't find it, Clark."

Clark slapped Eddy's hand. "I don't know who's been drinking out of this. You want me to get sick?"

The mug thumped on the thick white rug on the trailer floor, and coffee spattered everywhere. Eddy grabbed a napkin from the table and began to hastily dab at the stain. "It was clean."

I was shocked by Clark's behavior, but Manny looked almost bored as he turned on a laptop and tapped in a note. I supposed Clark lost his temper often. "One new rug," he said, and added as an afterthought, "but maybe we should make this one brown."

"I prefer white," Clark said, jiggling his leg nervously.

Manny glanced at him. "If your stomach's bothering you like you told me, maybe you shouldn't be drinking coffee."

Clark rubbed his stomach. "It was food poisoning. You should fire that caterer."

Manny sighed. "For the hundredth time, we have a contract with him."

"You lose me, you lose your show," Clark said.

"I wish you'd see a doctor, Clark," Manny grunted.

"I think it's an ulcer. No one else has gotten sick."

Eddy had gone back to the stove and was cooking some eggs. "No, no. I felt a little queasy too."

"You'd say anything for Clark." Manny looked at his watch. "Look at the time, Clark. You got to get into makeup. You ready, Tiger?"

"R-rowr," Clark growled.

I'd seen the same expression on Chris' face before a basketball game. He called it pumping himself up. The adrenaline would get going, and he'd get ready to focus on the game.

"Where's my jacket?" Clark asked.

"I'll get Wardrobe," Manny said, and he started for the door.

Clark scowled. "Eddy's supposed to do that. Eddy?"

Eddy came around the counter with a plate of eggs. "I was just finishing your scrambled eggs."

Clark bit off his words as if he could barely control himself. "I don't have time for them now."

"But you just said you wanted eggs," Eddy said stubbornly.

"You were too slow. I've got to shoot a scene. I need my jacket," Clark said.

"Jacket, right. Jacket." Eddy took a step toward a closet, stopped and pivoted, scanning the room. "Jacket, jacket," he muttered.

"That's your *job*, Eddy," Clark said.

"And I'm trying to do it," Eddy snapped. He started to cross the room, but he was in such a hurry that he bumped into Clark, spilling eggs all down Clark's T-shirt.

Clark stood for a moment, covered in eggs. Then he shouted at Eddy, "Can't you do anything without screwing up?"

"I'm sorry." Eddy snatched up a towel and began trying to wipe off the eggs.

Clark shoved him away so angrily that Eddy banged into the wall unit with the televisions.

"Sorry," Eddy whimpered.

Auntie tried to step in between them. "Clark didn't mean it, Eddy."

"Yeah, no prob," Manny said soothingly. "We got plenty of spares in Wardrobe."

Clark was too furious to hear anyone. "Can't you get anything right, you jerk?" He pushed Eddy so hard again that the televisions rocked.

"Sorry, sorry," Eddy said, raising his arms to protect his face.

"I'm always having to make excuses for your mistakes," Clark yelled. "If it wasn't for me, Manny would have fired you a long time ago."

Manny held up his hands, trying to look innocent. "Hey, now."

"Clark, don't get upset," Evie begged. "You've got to concentrate on your scene."

"You're right," Clark said. He reached out a hand to touch her cheek.

Chris jumped to his feet. "She's my girl, you ham," Chris said, stepping in between Clark and Evie.

Clark turned red with rage. "Who's a ham?"

"You are," Chris said. "You're nothing but a pretty face,

and your show's nothing but a piece of mind candy. You rot people's minds."

Clark shoved Chris. "I got the People's Choice award."

Chris was all wound up now. "People should be thinking about the world's real problems, like nuclear arms and pollution, not the toothpaste and the cars your dumb show pushes. You've got a lot to answer for."

"You're not really worried about saving the world. You're just jealous," Clark said, and he shoved Chris again.

"Quit that," Chris snarled.

"Who's going to make me?" Clark pushed him a third time.

This time Chris' fist connected with Clark's face, sending the heartthrob of millions backward into a chair. Chris seemed surprised he'd hit Clark, but I could see him puffing up like a peacock.

As he turned proudly toward Evie, though, she was already on her feet and running to Clark. "Clark, are you all right?"

That hurt Chris worse than any punch from Clark. "You're going to be sorry one day. Real sorry," he said, rubbing his knuckles. He glanced at Manny, who stepped back hurriedly.

"Chris," I said. I started to get up.

Auntie stopped me. "Let him cool off, kiddo."

Chris pointed a finger at Clark. "Gotcha," he said. Then with a swagger, he stepped outside.

When Manny and Eddy helped Clark sit up, I saw that Clark's million-dollar face had the mother of all shiners.

Manny stared at the black eye and then sighed. "Eddy,

get the makeup people in to start working on that eye," he said.

Eddy apologized: "It's all my fault, Clark. I should have stopped him."

"You've been protecting me since kindergarten. Aren't you getting tired of it?" Clark started to give his famous grin, but he stopped and winced at the pain.

Eddy smiled back. "You were the one who pushed me out of the way of that car and got a busted arm for your trouble."

Clark nodded in the direction of the shrine. "Cheated the Judge of the Dead."

"I've just been trying to pay you back," Eddy said.

"Get a spare T-shirt from Wardrobe, will you?" Manny asked.

"There's already an extra one in the trailer," Eddy said. He disappeared into the bedroom.

"If this gets into the tabloids next week, I'll know it's one of you," Clark said. He held up his fingers to form a rectangle. "I can just see the headlines: 'Fading Star Throws Tantrum.'"

"You're as big as ever," Manny assured him.

Clark shook his head. "It's been a disaster ever since they changed our time slot, but Warren and me are the ones they blame if we slip in the ratings." He got to his feet with Evie's and Auntie's help. "You know how it is, Tiger Lil."

"It's a lot of pressure," Auntie sympathized. "You feel like you're carrying the whole show on your shoulders; and if something goes wrong, it's your fault and nobody else's."

Eddy came out with a fresh T-shirt. "Here you go," he said, handing it to Clark.

I knew half of my school would have died to see Clark strip off his old T-shirt and put on a new one. "I'm sorry for blowing up at the kid, but Warren and I have been really stressed out since we slipped to number fourteen. The talk is that we're fading fast. That's another reason why he wants to jump into the movies, but this show is all I've got."

"Everyone's quick to dump on you," Auntie sympathized. Maybe she even identified with Clark's problems a little. I knew from what she had told me that she'd had her share of hard times in her own film career.

I thought of all the people I had seen. Their jobs—and the lives of their families—depended on Warren and Clark. That was a lot of responsibility for a teenager.

I tried to play the cheerleader. "But with Auntie involved, things are bound to head straight up."

"With a bullet." Clark grinned.

"A what?" I asked.

"When a record is hot on the charts, they put a symbol called a bullet beside it," Auntie explained.

"Let's hope I'm a prophet," Clark said.

We didn't realize just how much of one he was.

CHAPTER THREE

Wh^hen the makeup people came into the trailer with Eddy, they opened up their plastic cases, revealing enough jars and tubes and brushes to paint a wall mural rather than just Clark's face.

"What a day, and it's just starting." He closed his eyes as the makeup people started to work on his eye.

"Don't move a muscle on that face," one of the makeup people growled, and Clark's face froze.

He was just like a big doll. Maybe he had reason to be cranky.

"I wonder where Chris is," I whispered to Auntie.

"We'll go looking for him in a little bit," Auntie answered.

As the makeup people stepped back, Clark started to panic. "My jacket."

"Relax," Eddy said. "I remember now. When I got the spare T-shirt, I saw the jacket hanging on the back of the bedroom door." He brought it out and held it open for Clark.

"What would I do without you, Eddy?" Clark asked, shrugging into the jacket. "Get me some jook, will you. I think that's all my stomach can take right now."

Jook is a kind of rice porridge. It's good when you have stomach trouble and can't eat solid food.

Manny picked up his cell phone. "I'll alert security and have them escort that kid off the set."

"Clark," Auntie appealed to him.

Clark stood there while Eddy fussed over his costume. "No. Have them bring him to my trailer."

"Trying to win two falls out of three?" Manny asked.

"He's just a kid," Clark said. In fact, Chris was about his age, but Chris wasn't adored by millions.

Clark grinned apologetically at Evie. "It's not always like this."

I guess Evie was starstruck. "It's not your fault."

Clark clapped his hands together. "Well, let's get this show on the road."

"They should be ready," Manny said.

Only they weren't ready when we got to the front of the courthouse. By now, the sign and most of the front were hidden by a curtain of firecrackers. It looked like enough to blow up the front of the building.

A man sitting in a chair labeled DIRECTOR was arguing with a tall young Chinese while everyone else was standing around.

"And I want you to wear shades and a black leather coat."

"But it's so foggy that I don't need them," the young man said stubbornly. "And the coat's too hot."

"You look too . . . too preppy," the director said, waving a hand at the young man's clothes. "You've got to look like a hood."

"I didn't know that was the official uniform of a 'hood,'" the young man said.

As the two men argued, a chunky man in a dirty shirt came up with the biggest gun I had ever seen. On the T-shirt was the name Carl. With him was Chris, slouching along.

"We were worried about you. Where were you?" I demanded.

Carl jerked a thumb at Chris. "Does this duckling belong to you? He wandered into my prop room to ask for directions."

Chris shrugged sheepishly. "I couldn't find you when I went back to the trailer."

Auntie wrapped an arm around Chris. It looked affectionate enough, but I knew from Auntie's movies that she could quickly change it into a headlock. "Chris is going to behave, aren't you, Chris."

Chris glanced from Clark to Evie, but he didn't say anything.

"I'll leave you to your little soap opera later, boys and girls," Manny said, clapping his hands together. "Right now, I've got millions of people to entertain." He strode over toward the argument.

The director threw up his hands and turned around. "Manny, where did Casting find these louts? Get me some-one else. He's holding up the schedule. We've got to get this scene in the can."

The young man folded his arms. "I don't think that'd be a good idea."

"It's okay, Eng," Manny called to the young man, and he scooted over to the director, whispering urgently in his ear. I saw the director sulk. Then it was the young man's turn to be the target for Manny's charm. "It's been a hard shoot," he said to the young man. "He didn't mean anything by 'lout.'"

"I don't even know what it means." Eng frowned.

"This is acting," Manny coaxed. "You're not being you. You're being someone else."

"A hood in the official uniform," Eng said.

Manny spread his hands. "*You* might know hoods don't wear that stuff, but people around America don't know. The jacket, the shades. They're like signs. They say, 'Hey, this guy is tough. Don't mess with him.'"

"Like subtitling," Eng said, brightening.

"Exactly," Manny said.

The chunky man held up the gun. "Here's the prop. It's loaded with blanks, but I still think you ought to use one of the stunt guys."

Manny looked at the director. "I agree with Carl, Wayne." He nodded at Carl's back as he left.

Wayne slapped his hands on his sides in exasperation. "You get me more Asian stunt guys and that's fine. I'm tired of putting a wig on Raul and shooting him from behind every time we need a gag like this."

Eng looked at the gun distastefully. "And where am I supposed to keep that when I'm not shooting it off?"

"In a pocket," Wayne snapped.

Eng pointed at the long barrel. "It would never fit. It would just fall out."

Wayne ran a hand through his thinning hair. "In your pants then."

Eng was getting just as annoyed. "And ruin the lines of my clothing?"

Wayne rolled his eyes as if to say "Amateurs." But out loud, he said, "It doesn't matter. We'll let the audience use their imaginations about that. All they're going to see is you aiming and shooting."

Eng prodded the gun with a fingertip. "But real gang members wouldn't carry around a cannon like this. A cheap little police special does the job, and then you can throw it away."

"The gun is also like subtitling," Manny said.

"I'm going to feel silly," Eng said, but he took it.

"Millions of people will think you're the coolest, deadliest dude in the world," Manny coaxed.

Eng pressed his lips together tightly, looking as if he doubted that. Auntie and the rest of us retreated to the side while they ran through the scene. There was something that bugged me about the extras. Then I realized they were all boys, and they all looked just like they were fresh off the jet from China.

"There really ought to be some women," Auntie said to Manny.

Manny rubbed his chin. "Well . . . unh . . . we sort of went over budget. What you see here was all we could afford for the scene. And none of the boys would . . . um . . . dress as females."

Personally, I didn't see why he didn't get some new extras. "How about a camel?" I said.

"Why would we need one in Chinatown?" Manny wondered.

"I think she means a cameo," Auntie said, interpreting for me.

"It'd have to be for free," Manny warned.

"It'd be fun to see myself on the TV," Evie said, and she hooked an arm through Chris'. "Come on."

Chris shook free. "You know how I feel about this show," he said sullenly, and he jerked his head in Clark's direction. "And you know how I feel about him."

"It'll be just us girls then," Auntie said to Manny.

I thought we could just wear our regular clothes, but Manny wasn't having any of that. "This is Chinatown. You're too . . . too . . ."—He waved his hands in the air—"too contemporary."

Wardrobe had its own separate trailer, with smaller trailers for dressing rooms that everyone shared. The spare costumes were kept in a trailer that also doubled as the prop room. Though it was cool outside, the sun had already turned the prop trailer into a boiler, so the door had been left open. Looking through the doorway, we saw that it was a pack rat's nest of wigs, costumes, a stuffed lion and even a flying saucer.

Manny personally oversaw our transformation from real Chinatowners into television ones. Auntie put up with it because it was just one more costume. I didn't care because I'd be on television and could tell my friends. Evie, however, was upset after we changed in one of the dressing rooms.

She looked at her brown polyester slacks and pink-and-green floral-print blouse and wailed. "This is so . . . so . . ."

"Dowdy?" Auntie supplied.

Evie was holding her arms away from her sides as if the clothing were poisonous. "I look like someone's granny."

The wardrobe lady handed her a beat-up plastic shopping bag. "Now you do."

I pointed at Evie's own clothes, which had been hung up. "But that's what real Chinatowners wear."

"What are you?" Manny asked. "Second generation?"

"Third, actually," I said.

"Well, in our Chinatown—except for Clark—there are nothing but immigrants," Manny informed me.

"Hungry ones?" Auntie asked. I knew her well enough now to know she was looking for our motivation.

"Tired and worried as well as hungry," Manny suggested, shepherding us back to where they were shooting. "Got some more color for you," he told Wayne.

I thought Wayne, the harried director, would explode. Instead, he made a frame with his fingers and studied us through it. "Great. Just what we need."

So we began walking along the sidewalk with all the boys. We each had to set off at a different time so we would look like people who just happened to be passing by.

The directing had to be done through Eng, who translated into Chinese for the other extras.

"Remember: tired, worried, hungry," Auntie reminded us. Her shoulders slumped the next instant as if she had just worked a twelve-hour shift sewing in a sweatshop. I copied her posture and wrinkled up my face as if I were worried. That would be my addition to my character. Evie just walked along. I didn't see how she was ever going to win the role of Clark's girlfriend.

In the scene, Clark was strolling through a "typical" Chinatown crowd as Eng, the hired killer, stalked him.

Clark worked on the angle he used for his approach until the director was happy. On the sidewalk someone on the crew made chalk marks that would not be seen by the camera. Clark hit his mark and stopped, while Eng walked past his own mark.

So Wayne stopped us and had us rehearse it again. However, Eng was so nervous that he kept missing his mark.

"We got to get someone else," Wayne complained to Manny.

Eng started to look angry. Some of the boys did too. I supposed they were the ones who understood English, because once they whispered to the others in Chinese, the whole bunch looked mad.

Manny spoke urgently to Wayne, who began throwing sharp glances at Eng. Whatever Manny had said had changed Wayne's manner.

"I've just had a brainstorm," he said to Eng. "Why don't you wait in the courthouse? Then you come to the doorway. Clark will say his line, and then you shoot."

"It works for me," Clark said.

"I wonder what Manny said to Wayne," I said to Auntie.

Auntie chuckled like an old veteran. "Manny probably

told him that Eng was some relation to a sponsor. I remember this one Hercules film we were shooting in Italy. The producer bribed some museum guard and got real swords for everyone. The stunt guys were fine, but there was this one kid—the son of one of the backers—who got carried away and nearly took off someone's head. We had to stop production for half a day while they found a rubber sword for him."

The next time, the run-through went all right. Clark hit his mark and stared at the courthouse. Eng came to the doorway.

"Gotcha," Clark said, pointing his finger like a gun.

Then Eng lifted his gun from his side and aimed at Clark.

"Two hands, two hands," Wayne screamed. "Remember what we taught you?" He leaped from his chair and bent his legs, holding one wrist with his other hand as he pretended to aim.

Eng rested his gun on his shoulder. "That's silly. Do you want me to show you how a 'hood' really shoots?" he asked lazily.

Wayne suddenly grew very pale. "That won't be necessary."

We shot the scene for real. It had been easy during the rehearsal to pretend to be an immigrant girl. However, when the cameras were rolling for real, it got the juices going, and I forgot what I was supposed to be. Of course, Auntie, like the professional she was, was the exact same as in rehearsal. Evie was still walking as stiffly as a zombie, though. I didn't see how she'd ever win an audition.

Clark stopped in his spot and faced the courthouse. Eng, looking nervous, stepped out.

Clark spoke his trademark line and aimed his finger.

Licking his lips, Eng raised his pistol. It shook badly. For all his bravado with the director, he was having heebie-jeebies once the cameras started rolling. I figured we were going to have to reshoot the scene. After all, he was supposed to be a cold-blooded assassin.

A stuntman set off the firecrackers. There were little flashes of light, and pungent streams of smoke suddenly rose upward. Next to me, Evie had covered her ears against the explosions. I almost did the same thing, but I thought about the camera. Auntie had taught me to be a trouper.

As firecrackers banged and showered the sidewalk with shredded red paper, Clark started to duck on cue as Eng pulled the trigger.

Suddenly there was a bigger, brighter flash of light, but the sound of the blank going off was masked by the firecrackers.

The next moment the streetlamp exploded.

Auntie gasped. "Duck! He's shooting real bullets!"

CHAPTER FOUR

Eng dropped the pistol like it was a snake that had just bitten him, but it was already too late. "Get the cops! He tried to kill Clark," Wayne shouted.

"No, I didn't mean it!" Eng said, holding up his hands.

The cops from the barricades had come running. Officer Quan was in the lead.

Wayne grabbed him as he passed and pointed at Eng. "He just tried to shoot my star."

"What do you expect when you hire the Powell Street Boys?" Officer Quan shouted angrily, and he pulled himself free.

Suddenly I understood the sour comments he had made at the barricades.

Lately, if you read any news about Chinatown, it was usually bad, and the Powell Street boys were right in the middle of it. They were a gang that had been trying to establish themselves by grabbing attention—and anything else they could get their hands on.

He must have hated seeing them running loose on the set.

When the Powell Street Boys saw the cops coming, they started to head for Eng. Some of them were pulling guns out of their jacket or pants pockets—and theirs would also have real bullets.

Officer Quan grabbed a radiophone from its clip on his shoulder and began speaking into it urgently. "We need backup," he started.

Looking scared but determined, the boys formed a small ring around Eng. "What're the Powell Street Boys doing here?" I asked Auntie.

"It happens all the time on films," Auntie explained. "Sometimes the only way a film company can insure peace is to hire the toughest gang. When they shoot in New York around Times Square, you can have twice as many 'drivers' as you have trucks."

"That's why they were hired as the crowd," I said. "Well, the Powell Street Boys always seem to want headlines. This'll certainly get everyone's attention."

"But you usually don't want your crime recorded on film," Auntie said thoughtfully, "and with dozens of cops around."

Eng was still in the middle of the street protesting his innocence, while his gang had gathered around him. At the same time, the cops were starting to close in.

"Get out." Officer Quan started to wave his arm at the crew. Some of them were starting to duck for cover, but I noticed Manny grabbing the cameraman and holding him in position. And all Wayne had done was duck behind his chair—though I didn't see what protection the cloth back would give him from a bullet. In the middle of the street, Clark seemed to come out of his daze. Turning, he ran behind the nearest trailer.

In a moment, there woud be another bunch of explosions, but they wouldn't be firecrackers. These would be bullets.

"Get in a doorway, kiddo." Auntie shoved me toward a building.

I started to back up, but then I saw Auntie was going forward instead. "Auntie, where are you going?"

"To stop a bloodbath," Auntie said, and she trotted through the police line before anyone could stop her.

"Is your aunt crazy?" Evie asked.

"Only some of the time," I said. I just wished this weren't one of those occasions.

"*Wait*," Auntie said in Chinese to the gang, and then she turned to face the cops. "Wait. I saw him. He didn't know he was shooting real bullets."

"Then he won't mind coming in to answer a few questions," Officer Quan said tensely.

Eng was feeling a little tougher now that he was surrounded by his gang. "No way," he yelled. "I've been framed."

Auntie was holding out her arms with the palms flattened perpendicular to the ground. "They got the whole scene on film. You looked as surprised as the rest of us. You didn't know you were shooting live ammunition."

"Yeah," Eng said, shouting to the cops. "Look at the film."

"You still have to come in to the station," Officer Quan said.

By now, most of the street had cleared except for the little bunch around the camera. Manny practically had a headlock around the neck of the cameraman to keep him there. I wished Auntie would have the sense to clear out as well. Real bullets wouldn't bounce off her.

"You're too smart to get everyone killed," Auntie coaxed Eng. "And that's just what's going to happen if you don't go with the police."

At that moment, though, the old man we had seen earlier shuffled out of the laundry. "Eng, *behave yourself. You obey the lady,*" he scolded in Chinese.

Eng didn't turn around, but he answered in Chinese. "*Get out of here, Grandpa. You could get hurt.*"

That didn't stop the little old man. He forced his way through the outer ring of cops and kept on right toward the gang. "*Don't you recognize her? That's Tiger Lil.*"

"*So what, Grandpa?*" Eng asked, annoyed.

"*If she says you'll be safe, then you will be,*" the old man said, and he shoved between the gang members. "*She's a big film star.*"

"*Who cares?*" Eng snapped.

Grandpa Eng had to almost stand on tiptoe to slap his grandson on the ear. "*You may not respect me, but you respect her.*"

Eng crouched, holding his ear. "*Ow, Grandpa. That hurt.*"

Grandpa Eng sternly held up a hand. "*Maybe if I had done that when you were small, you might not have turned out so rotten and spoiled. Now you listen to the lady."*

"But Grandpa . . ." Eng protested like a small boy.

There were a few chuckles from the gang as well as the police.

"You mind her," Grandpa Eng said, pointing toward Auntie. *"Go."*

"Don't you understand?" Eng asked in frustration. *"The cops'll pin this on me. They've been looking for an excuse to get me."*

Grandpa Eng lowered his voice. *"Whatever else happens to you, I don't want you dead. Or any of your friends, or anyone else."* He waved an arm around to include the street. *"You're too smart for that. I taught you how to play the percentages. If you resist, you and all your friends will lose. And so will a lot of other people."*

Eng listened to the sound of sirens. The police were getting more reinforcements. *"Why should I listen to an old booze hound?"*

Grandpa Eng winced, but he said, *"It's too early for even me to be drunk. I swear I won't let them keep you in jail long."*

Eng smiled sadly at his grandfather. *"You haven't had too good a record at keeping your word."*

Embarrassed, Grandpa Eng dipped his head. *"I know I've let you down a lot in the past. But this is one time I won't."*

Eng laughed harshly. *"You old booze hound, you're still talking big and making promises you can't keep."* Then he took a deep breath and pulled back his shoulders. *"But what kind of man lets his friends die for him?"*

Grandpa Eng patted him on the back. *"Good boy."*

Eng held up his hands again. "Don't shoot. I'm giving up."

He walked between the other gang members, and Grandpa Eng followed, escorting him to Officer Quan.

"I'll see you real soon," Grandpa Eng said. *"Then I'll treat you to a nice dinner."*

"Yeah, right," Eng said skeptically.

As Officer Quan handcuffed him, the rest of the Powell Street boys split. I tried to get to Auntie, but I felt like a salmon swimming upstream. "How many times do I have to tell you? You don't have your stunt double anymore. You can't go charging out like that."

Manny hurried toward Clark, and the rest of the crew came out of hiding. Auntie let out her breath in a rush. "I'd rather have a script for a scene like that than have to ad lib."

"I'm going to get you a bulletproof vest for Christmas." I gave her a hug.

"Oof," Auntie grunted. "You're squeezing a little too tight if you just want to get my measurements." But she returned my hug. I guessed she had been scared after all.

Finally she let go of me. "Now come on, kiddo. We've got to solve this case for Chris," she said.

"What for? Eng took the shot," I said.

"You saw his face. He didn't know the gun was loaded," Auntie said. "Once the cops figure that out, guess who's next on their list."

I thought of the cop shows I had watched. Who else had the means, the opportunity, and the motive? My big dumb brother, Chris. Evie was motive enough; and as proof of that, he had hit Clark and then made threats. Chris had also been in the prop room. Unfortunately, that gave him the opportunity.

"Chris wouldn't do it," I said.

"You know it, and I know it, but will the cops know it?" Auntie asked grimly.

"Well, how would he know the gun was going to be shot at Clark?" I asked.

"Let's ask Carl," Auntie said, "but you heard how he was bragging about the gun just a moment ago. Some people are proud of what they do and like to let everyone know it."

"*Excuse me,*" Grandpa Eng asked shyly in Chinese. "*Aren't you Tiger Lil?*"

When I let go of Auntie, I saw him standing a few feet away. He was hurriedly trying to straighten his clothes.

"Yes," Auntie said.

"*I have heard from Mrs. Chin. You helped her at the sweat-shop,*" Grandpa Eng said. That had been our first case, when we had found the stolen pearls. "*And I also happen to know Ah Luke.*" We'd met him during Auntie's second case, when she had tried to find some stolen money.

"*Yes; how are they?*" Auntie asked politely.

"*They are fine. They both told me you fixed things,*" the old man said.

"*We just got lucky,*" Auntie said modestly.

Grandpa Eng's faith in Auntie was touching. "*Then you must have a lot of luck,*" he said. "*So will you help my grandson?*"

"*What he needs is a good lawyer,*" Auntie said.

"Lawyers are expensive," Grandpa Eng said, "and I have no money."

"Well, there are public defenders. I'll see what I can do about getting him a good one," Auntie promised.

"But he'll need more," Grandpa Eng insisted. "You're a Chinatown girl, so I know I can trust you. Please promise me that you'll help."

Auntie hesitated. "Really, you need someone else."

I saw shiny tears in the corners of Grandpa Eng's eyes. "I know he's done wrong, but a lot of that's my fault. I don't have anyone to turn to except you."

Auntie put her hand on his shoulder. "It may not be enough, but I'll try my best."

He squeezed Auntie's hand in his own. "That's all I can ask."

"Where can I reach you?" Auntie asked.

He nodded toward the laundry. "The boss lets me sleep there. Dirty laundry makes a smelly bed, but a soft one."

And then he turned in time to see to his grandson being led away. "Wait, wait," he called, waving his hand.

Officer Quan would have stopped, but the grandson kept moving. Since Officer Quan had kept hold of his arm, Eng actually pulled the policeman along. "Don't pay him any attention," Eng said bitterly in English.

Grandpa Eng paused in midstep. His hand slowly dropped to his side. "I just got you help."

Eng continued to move. "He's just an old drunk. Lots of promises, but no delivery."

"Guess who just got to be Federal Express," Auntie muttered.

"Can you deliver?" I asked.

"I don't know," Auntie said, giving her head a shake. Then she leaned forward determinedly, the way she had in her movie *Tiger Lil to the Rescue*. "But I'm sure going to give it a good try. It looks like we're working to save not only Grandpa Eng's grandson, but Chris as well."

I just hoped we could.

CHAPTER FIVE

The trouble was that my goofball brother didn't believe he was in any danger. "I didn't touch the gun. I wouldn't know where to put the bullets."

"The cops don't know that," Auntie snapped. "I've got to call up Charley Moy right away."

"Who's that?" I asked.

"One of the best lawyers around," Auntie said. "He's become a big-league hitter, but he's always kept his office in Chinatown."

"I don't need a lawyer," Chris insisted.

"There's a difference between justice and our legal system, kiddo," Auntie said. "I found that out with my first film contract."

As we walked toward the makeshift dressing room, Chris studied Auntie. "I'm still shaking. You could have been killed."

Evie shook her head. "That was the bravest thing I ever saw," she gushed.

"Or the stupidest," Chris said. "He was shooting real bullets."

"If he'd shot me, he'd have done what the film critic for *The New York Times* wanted to do thirty years ago." Auntie shrugged.

"How can you make jokes?" Chris asked, puzzled. "You just prevented a massacre!"

"What's the life of one old ham against the lives of all these people?" Auntie said.

"I just stood there, but you did something," Chris said. He seemed upset with himself.

I poked him in the ribs. "What do you expect? She's Tiger Lil."

Bad choice to call attention to myself. Auntie looked at me. "I don't suppose I can talk you into going home. Things might get rough."

"Our first two cases were pretty rough too," I said. "You needed me on both."

"I don't want you getting hurt on my account," Chris said, suddenly worried. "So just forget it."

"Even if you weren't involved, we have a client," I explained. "Eng's grandfather asked her to help."

Chris folded his arms in disapproval. "It looks like Eng's a real gangster. How can you help him? I mean, even if he didn't plan to kill Clark, he's probably done enough bad stuff to deserve jail."

"Probably," Auntie agreed, "but this is America, kiddo. You don't get convicted for your reputation. You only go to prison if you're found guilty of a specific crime."

I wasn't too keen on helping Eng either, but I had to

admit Auntie was right. "Even if you weren't involved, we'd have to solve the case just to be fair."

"Why risk your neck for someone like that?" Chris asked, puzzled.

"You're always talking about fighting injustice," I said, bristling. "Well, this is a perfect example of it. You can't just pick and choose about justice."

Looking sheepish, Chris ran his hand through his hair. "I guess."

Auntie watched Grandpa Eng shuffle back toward the laundry. "Besides, it's not for Eng. It's for that old man. Look at him. He's probably never been paid a decent wage in his life or had a decent meal or a suit of clothes. And yet he'll work till he drops. It's men like that who built America."

Ashamed, Chris fingered the buttons of his shirt. "I didn't think about that."

"I guess you can't blame Grandpa Eng for drinking," I said.

"You're always talking about 'the people' and how we have to help them," Auntie explained gently. "Well, sometimes you have to do it one person at a time."

And if anyone could do it, my auntie could—with my help.

When we got to the trailer, Evie wagged her index finger at Chris in a mock scolding. "Now don't you go wandering off again."

Chris got that goofy grin again. "I'll be guarding the door."

As we changed inside, Evie asked anxiously, "Chris

53

will be all right, won't he?"

"We'll see to it," Auntie said, buttoning her blouse.

"He seemed pretty mad," Evie said, biting her lip. "And he told Clark he'd be sorry."

"After seeing Clark Tom in operation, I think a lot of boyfriends probably have said the same thing," Auntie said.

Evie blushed. "I was just flattered. It didn't mean anything."

We'd see what the cops thought, though.

"So where do we start?" I asked as we stepped outside.

"I think we visit the prop room," Auntie said.

Chris rubbed his knuckles. One lucky punch and he thought he was a superhero. "I'm going along too. I'm sorry that I wasn't much help with Eng."

"You don't have anything to prove to anyone, kiddo," Auntie said. "We can take care of ourselves."

Chris tousled my hair. "No, you're right, Auntie. How can I help the world if I can't help one old man? Besides, what about the shrimp? She's a nuisance, but she's *my* nuisance."

Carl was inside the prop room. It was stuffed with props, but I saw costumes, too, and even a clothes hamper. Maybe Wardrobe used it for a storeroom too. He was eating from one of the white boxes of food that seemed to be everywhere. He had improvised a table out of a stuffed lion. "Go away. I'm on my break," he said when we poked our heads inside.

"Didn't you hear the shooting?" Auntie asked.

Carl laughed. "There's always a lot of shooting. Whenever Wayne can't figure out how to end a scene, he has someone get shot. We call him Commander Boom-Boom."

"Well, there was a real bullet in the prop gun," Auntie said.

"Not in my gun," Carl insisted.

"It's on film," Auntie told him. "The cops will probably be wanting to talk to you next."

"Did anyone get hurt?" he demanded, suddenly worried.

"A streetlamp died," Auntie said.

"I loaded that gun myself with blanks, and it never left this room until I brought it to the set," Carl said as he bit into a bagel.

"Did you talk to Chris about the gun?" Auntie asked.

Carl chewed thoughtfully. "Yeah, but you know how boys are. They see a big gun, and it's like a toy they got to know all about."

"Did you leave the prop room for any reason before you brought the gun to the set?" Auntie asked.

"Nope, I had to get things ready for the next scene and another one," Carl said. "The next scene is a really tricky one. Watch Leo." When he kicked the lion, its eyes suddenly lit up and started to blink, while its tongue flicked out and then in, out and in.

I didn't understand what Carl meant about the next scene. It didn't make sense to me. "What does a stuffed lion have to do with a shootout?"

"In film and even in television, they don't shoot all the scenes in sequence. They shoot them by location because it's cheaper. Then they edit them later and put them in the proper chronological order," Auntie explained.

55

"So we'll do the beginning and the end of the show here," Carl added. "Then the editor will put all the footage together later."

"How do you keep track of it all?" I asked.

"It's not easy," Carl said.

"It's not easy trying to get into the mood of a scene either," Auntie said.

I could see that was true, if one scene required you to be sad and the next one to be happy.

"Well," Evie asked, "shouldn't they reshoot the scene—pardon the pun—with new actors?"

Carl went back to tinkering with Leo. "Naw, from what I remember of the script, the kid was only in that scene. They can edit things so you don't see Clark flinch or the streetlamp explode. Knowing Manny, he's probably planning some big publicity campaign about how true crime comes to prime time."

Auntie watched the lion perform for a moment. "I can't wait to see this episode on television."

"You and a chunk of the country," Carl said, "but I won't be one of them. Give me films any day."

"You can take your time on films. Maybe shoot just one scene a day," Auntie said.

"Instead of bunches," Carl said. "Our Fearless Leader likes just one take, and then it's on to the next." He nodded to Auntie. "You in the film business?"

"This is Tiger Lil," I said. "She's made lots of movies."

Carl stopped chewing. "I thought you looked familiar. *Gore Galore*, right?"

"Yes." Auntie grinned. "It took me weeks to wash the blood out of my hair."

"I know two actors who changed to being redheads after that," Carl teased.

"I should have done that too." Auntie laughed. "Say, Carl. Did anyone visit you before you delivered the prop gun?"

"Just the lost duckling here." Carl nodded to Chris.

My brother was capable of a lot of things, but not a murder attempt. The trouble was: I believed in him, but would the cops? After all, he'd had that fight with Clark over Evie and then made what sounded like a threat.

Auntie started to look worried. "You said you were working on Leo. Where was the gun?"

Carl jerked a thumb behind him. "On the table."

I glanced at Auntie. "So you had your eye off the gun?"

Carl stared up at the ceiling, from which hung a variety of rubber chickens. "I guess."

Evie put a hand over her mouth. "Then someone could have put a bullet in the gun."

All this time Leo had kept on blinking his eyes and sticking out his tongue. Carl gave Leo another kick. "Come on. Quit it, Leo,"

As we stepped outside, Officer Quan saw us. Hitching up his belt, he headed over toward us. "I'm looking for Evie."

Evie reluctantly raised her hand. "Here."

Officer Quan nodded to Chris. "And you're Chris?"

Chris gulped. "Yes."

"Do you mind answering a few questions?" Officer

Quan asked Evie, but it was a command rather than a request. Then he jerked his head at Chris. "Stick around where we can find you. I know the D.A.'s going to have questions."

Evie walked toward him as if she were heading toward her own funeral.

"That settles it," Auntie said, fishing some change from her purse. She slipped away to find a pay telephone.

As Evie was being interviewed, Chris had a worried look. "Do you think I'm going to be in trouble? I mean, I did say 'you're going to be sorry'—but I meant Evie would be sorry she lost me."

"Too late for footnotes," I said. "You should have watched what you said."

Chris jammed his hands into his pockets. "Yeah," he said glumly.

Still looking worried, Auntie joined us. "Charley's coming right away. You're not to say a thing until he gets here."

Chris slouched against the side of the prop trailer. "I told you. I don't need him." But he didn't sound so sure anymore.

When Officer Quan let Evie go, she looked sad. "I couldn't help it, Chris. I had to tell him what you said about Clark being sorry and all."

Chris closed his eyes. "I was telling you that you'd be sorry if you stuck with him."

Evie put a hand over her mouth. "Oh, no. Let me talk to him again."

Chris took her hand and tried to put on a brave face.

"It'll be okay. I've got nothing to hide. Are you really worried about me?"

Big brothers. If I were facing a charge of attempted murder, I'd think about more things than Evie's pretty brown eyes. I felt like kicking him, but I knew it would take more than a swift kick to put some sense into him.

"Well, sort of," Evie said.

Not exactly a love sonnet, but then brains weren't Evie's best asset.

As the two lovebirds gazed into each other's eyes, Auntie got down to the important things. Sniffing the air, she patted her stomach. "You know, all this detecting has worked up my appetite."

It didn't take detecting alone to work up her appetite, but my stomach was starting to growl. I remembered that I hadn't had any breakfast. "Me too."

Everywhere on the set, crewmembers were eating from white boxes. None of them seemed worried about food poisoning. "Where do you get one of those food boxes?"

"The caterer must be around here somewhere," Auntie said. She snagged Chris' and Evie's arms. "Come on, you two. You need to eat something."

Evie giggled. "I'm not hungry, but I'll keep you company."

Chris was looking a little stupider than usual. "You're not afraid to be near a possible suspect?"

"I know you're innocent," Evie said.

I made gagging noises, but Auntie just laughed. "You just wait. That's going to be you in six years."

"Never," I swore, and I whispered to Auntie, "Couldn't

we just leave them behind? I think they'd rather be alone."

"Without a chaperone?" Auntie asked. "No way."

We found the caterer's white van parked behind another trailer. On its side was a sign: QUALITY CATERING. On a long table outside were stacks of more white boxes as well as large metal urns marked COFFEE, DECAF, and HOT WATER. There were also pitchers of orange juice and bottles of chilled water.

One of the caterers must have had a sense of humor, because someone had put up a sign saying: PICK YOUR POISON.

"Just look like you belong, kiddo," Auntie whispered. We joined a line of people and each took a box, even Chris. I guess he looked like just another Chinatown extra, because no one protested. As we retreated with our loot, Auntie said, "There's just the person to talk to." Suddenly she began waving her bagel in the air. "Yo, Norm!"

CHAPTER SIX

We were standing near Clark's trailer when I saw Norm working his way across the set. I thought of Manny's observation. Norm really did look like he should be selling shoes instead of putting evildoers behind bars. His real love, though, was acting, and he worked at it part-time. He had signed up as one of Auntie's first clients.

He stopped when he heard Auntie. "Are you here as an actor, an agent, or a detective, Tiger Lil?"

"A little of all three," Auntie said, bustling over.

"Well, I can only talk to the first two," Norm said, and he nodded to me. "How're you doing, Lily?"

"Fine now that I got some food," I said. "I never get to eat regularly when I'm with Auntie."

"There's always a little too much excitement when your aunt's around," Norm agreed.

"Speaking of which, who's the best public defender, Norm?" Auntie asked.

"So you're representing Eng," Norm said. "But how? As an actor or an accused murderer?"

"He's no murderer, Norm," Auntie said. "He didn't know the gun was loaded."

"That has yet to be determined," Norm said carefully.

"But what's his motive?" I demanded.

"You've corrupted her innocent mind," Norm accused Auntie.

Auntie tapped her heart. "I'll answer for it in heaven. I'd still like the name of the best person in the public defender's office."

"I can't discuss the case with you," Norm said primly. "But may I remind you that we have film of him actually shooting at Clark?"

"Maybe he was framed," Auntie argued. "You ought to check into that."

"We will, but I might remind you of this, too: He's a known criminal with a record two inches thick," Norm said.

Auntie narrowed her eyes. "Are you really going to be thorough? Or are you just going to give the appearance of being thorough? His grandfather's afraid that your boss is going to railroad Eng into prison," she said.

"I wouldn't suggest that anything like that could happen in our well-honed legal system," Norm said.

Auntie must have detected something in his tone. "Are you telling me Eng's in trouble?" she demanded.

"Perish forbid," Norm said, but he looked grim.

Auntie wagged her bagel at him. "I hope you're ready to audition for nothing but dog food commercials."

Norm rubbed his head unhappily. "I'm just trying to do my job."

Auntie planted her fists on her hips. "And wait until you see me do mine."

"Have a heart. I'm allergic to dogs, Tiger Lil," Norm protested.

"Heh, heh, heh," Auntie chuckled evilly.

Norm tilted up his head with great dignity. "If all I do is audition for dog food commercials after this, so be it. There's no such thing as a small part—"

"Only small actors," Auntie finished.

"I suppose I look like a suspect too," Chris said, and he bit his lip. From the guilty way he looked, you would have thought he was an ax murderer.

"Why?" Norm demanded.

"I . . . I decked Clark Tom," Chris blurted out. "I thought he was making a pass at my . . . unh . . . friend."

Evie giggled. "Oh, Chris. You got it all wrong."

Norm took her in with one glance and then turned back to Chris. "Who're you?" Norm asked.

"My nephew, Chris," Auntie explained. "He's Lily's brother."

"Well, giving you the name of a good public defender would be a conflict of interest," Norm said, and pulled an invisible zipper across his mouth. "My lips are sealed."

Auntie folded her arms. "That would be fine if we lived in a fair city where the higher-ups wouldn't use that as an excuse to railroad him into a prison cell."

"No, we wouldn't," Norm said dryly.

"That would leave the real would-be murderer still on the loose," Auntie said, taking a bite from her bagel, "and free to try again."

Norm glanced sympathetically at Chris. He must have thought we wanted a lawyer for my brother. "Well, the one person I'd hate to tangle with in a court is Cynthia Patel," Norm said. "But that's my secret."

"I won't tell anyone," Auntie said.

Norm prodded Chris' chest with his forefinger. "So you'd better call Ms. Patel now, young fellow. I want to talk to you."

"I don't need a lawyer," Chris said. "I've got nothing to hide."

Norm turned to Auntie. "Those are famous last words, Tiger Lil. Better get him representation."

"Get off the set," Manny said. He charged toward us. "Don't I have enough trouble without your bringing on your clients?"

Norm looked puzzled. "How do you know me? We've never met."

"Tiger Lil gave me your glossy," Manny said, and he turned to an assistant. "Steve, get the cops."

Auntie cleared her throat. "Norm only acts part-time. He's here in his other capacity."

"I'm with the district attorney's office," Norm said, taking out a card.

"Assistant district attorney, huh?" Manny flipped the card back and forth over a fingernail thoughtfully. I don't think he cared about Norm's acting ability, but it would be handy for a film company to have friends in high places. Turning to Auntie, he was all smiles. "Who else have you got on your client list?"

"I've got some real gems," Auntie said, suddenly coy.

64

"I'll take another look at that file," Manny said, interested.

"Even if you hire me, don't expect any special favors," Norm warned.

"No, no, of course not," Manny said, tapping the card against Norm's chest. "A man like you has too much integrity. Have you had any breakfast?"

"I have to talk to the investigating officers," Norm said.

Manny, though, had already slung an arm around his shoulders and was steering him toward the catering table. "They can have breakfast too."

At that moment, Wayne came up. "Manny, we got a problem."

"Not now," Manny snapped.

"Clark won't do the next shot," Wayne complained.

Manny slapped his forehead and then in the wink of an eye was all smiles again. "Why don't you help yourself to a meal, Norm? I can call you Norm, can't I?"

Norm didn't say anything as he headed off. I guess he had on his district-attorney hat today rather than his actor's hat.

That didn't stop Manny, though. He waved a good-bye to Norm's back. "Right, Norm. We'll talk later."

At that moment a pale Clark came walking toward his trailer. "I'm done for the day, Manny."

"What's the big idea, Clark?" Manny said, pouncing on him.

"In case you didn't notice, I've just been shot at," Clark snapped. He was still in costume.

"But they got him," Manny said.

"He's also got a gang," Clark said. "And there were too many for the cops to catch them all."

A guilty big brother was worse than a big brother on his high horse. Chris cleared his throat. "I'm sorry. You know I didn't mean anything when I tried to hit you."

It took Clark a moment to recognize Chris. I think Auntie's suspicions were right about Clark making a lot of boyfriends jealous. "Sure, kid." Then he saw Evie. He recognized her more quickly. "You're a lucky girl to have someone care about you like that."

"I guess." Evie giggled nervously.

I could see Clark's charm going into automatic. I don't think he could help it any more than a bird can help singing or the sun can help rising.

Fortunately Manny intervened before Chris could get jealous again. "Clark, the show must go on."

"Save that for Ethel Merman," Clark snapped.

I glanced at Auntie. "An old-time musical star," she whispered.

At that moment, Eddy ran up eagerly, balancing a big Styrofoam soup container. "I got the jook you wanted."

"With the preserved egg?" Clark asked.

"I . . . I forgot," Eddy said, hanging his head.

"Geez, Eddy. You keep making one mistake after another," Clark said in exasperation.

I didn't remember Clark asking for any such thing. "I'll get it right this time," Eddy promised, and he scurried away.

As Clark stalked to his trailer—followed by a pleading

Manny—I whispered to Auntie, "What was Norm really trying to say?"

"That I might disappoint Grandpa Eng," Auntie said grimly.

"But if Eng didn't do it, then maybe the cops will think Chris did," I said.

Chris was stunned. "You don't think that I could do that."

Auntie sighed. "Listen to your old auntie, Chris. You're next in line after Eng on the list of suspects."

"Am I in that much trouble, Auntie?" Chris looked scared now.

Auntie gave him a quick, reassuring hug. "Don't worry. We'll get you out of this, kiddo."

We'd have to. Bullets or not.

CHAPTER SEVEN

Charley Moy looked like a beach ball on stilts. His torso was short and out of proportion to his long legs.

"I don't need you," Chris tried to insist. I guess he was still clinging to the belief that everyone would see his innocence.

"Shut up, Macho Man," Auntie said, and she brought Charley up to speed. Then Charley went over the details with Chris—though he practically had to pry the information out of him.

When Officer Quan finally came to take Chris over to Norm, Charley greeted him. "Haven't seen you in a while."

Officer Quan looked like he had just dipped his head in a pickle barrel. "Not since you took me apart on the witness stand."

"No hard feelings?" Charley said. He searched his memory. "Officer Quan, right? Just doing my job."

"She stole that television," Officer Quan said. "I caught her with it in her arms."

Charley shrugged. "That's not what the jury thought." He explained to Auntie. "It was an alimony case. It turned out that the television belonged to her."

"She had no right to take it before the final settlement," Officer Quan snapped.

Charley chuckled. "Who'd have thought a teeny woman like that could carry a thirty-inch television set? Don't you think that proved the righteousness of her cause?"

Officer Quan broke into a smile. "A modern version of trial by combat."

As the two reminisced, a slouching Chris trailed them.

Evie looked worried as she watched Chris go off with Charley and Officer Quan. "Is Chris going to be okay?" she asked.

I gave her points for being concerned about my brother.

"I'm sure he'll be fine," Auntie said—though she looked just as anxious. "I just wish he hadn't been in that prop room."

"It's all my fault," Evie said, biting a nail. There went her manicure.

"Don't blame yourself. Males can't help being males." Auntie sighed. "However, we're definitely going to give the police a little help."

I grinned. "Whether they want it or not."

Auntie chewed her lip. "First things first. Let's find out the real reason Manny hired Eng and his gang."

I thought Manny would be watching Clark in the middle of his scene with Leo. However, the whole crew was standing around in frustration while Clark and Manny stood outside Clark's trailer, arguing.

"Where's Leo?" I whispered to Auntie.

"I don't see him. They must be shooting another scene for some reason," Auntie murmured back.

Manny was pleading with his star, "Look, Clark. I've got to replace all the extras because they ran off once the police showed up, so we can only shoot certain scenes. We can't fall behind. I've doubled security. You're safer than the President of the United States now."

At first my sympathies were with Clark. If I'd had someone shoot at me, I wouldn't want to be the center of attention either.

"You can't even provide me with a safe meal. How can you provide me with protection?" Clark demanded.

Manny screwed his eyes shut, squeezed his hands into fists, and thrust them up in the air. "Why didn't I become a dentist like my mother wanted?"

"I'm going to change. Then I'm returning to the hotel," Clark said.

"I'll triple security," Manny offered.

Clark hesitated, and then he got a gleam in his eyes. "There's still the food."

Manny took out a small cell phone from his pocket. "All right. I'll call the production company's lawyers and get them to cancel the contract."

"When?" Clark demanded.

Manny flipped open the phone. "After this week."

"'Bye," Clark said, and turned.

Manny began to hit himself over the head with his cell

phone. "If it isn't disappearing extras, it's firecrackers; and if it isn't firecrackers, it's lions; and if it isn't lions, it's real bullets. And if it isn't bullets, it's temperamental stars."

"Who have targets on their backs," Clark said as he walked away.

"Hold it." Rubbing the sore spot, Manny punched in a phone number and began to talk to someone. "Tomorrow okay?" he asked Clark.

When Clark hesitated, Auntie said, "No one's gotten sick so far today. The crew needs to eat. You've got Eddy to fetch stuff for you, but what will they do?"

Clark rubbed his chin. "I guess so."

Manny spoke urgently into the phone and then put it away. "Today is the last day you'll see them. You know I'll do anything for you, Clark. You're my star. Come on. Let me show you the new security precautions."

Auntie plucked at his sleeve. "Excuse me, Manny."

"What?" Manny asked in annoyance. "I'm busy."

Now that Chris' safety was involved, Manny might as well have tried to stop a tank. "I couldn't help wondering why you hired a gang as extras," Auntie said.

That gave Manny something new to rant about. "I wish I'd never written about them. I wish I'd never written the first script for this show. I wish I'd never bought a type-writer."

His curses might have gone back to the creation of the world if Auntie hadn't given him a shake. "Manny, what about the gang?"

Clark folded his arms. "I'm curious too."

"Well, you know we need a lot of firecrackers for

71

Commander Boom-Boom." He shot a sour look in Wayne's direction. "I'd gotten a really good deal on a whole load of firecrackers, but then the Powell Street Boys told me this was their turf and I had to buy from them. So I not only had to cancel the other deal and get the firecrackers from them, but I also had to hire the whole bunch of them for that scene to make up for insulting them."

"Maybe we can help Grandpa Eng after all," Auntie said to me, and then she asked Manny, "Who was the first dealer?"

"Some fast-talking kid called Nick," Manny said. "Now if you'll excuse me, I have to go slit my throat."

"Clark's a pro. He'll get everything in one take and put you back on schedule," Auntie assured him.

"Gotcha," Clark said to Auntie.

"That's my guy," Manny said, throwing an arm around Clark.

As Manny hustled his star away, I grabbed Auntie excitedly. "Do you think Nick could have framed Eng?"

"It would be a good way of getting even with Eng for taking over the job," Auntie said.

"But how did the dealer get the real bullets into the gun?" Evie asked. "Carl said the only ones who came in were Chris and the wardrobe people."

Auntie snapped her fingers. "Wait a moment. Carl was eating from a catering box."

"So did all the extras and most of the crew," I said.

"But he also said he never left the prop room," Auntie said. "And yet we had to go to the table. So how did he get the food?"

"Maybe somebody brought it to him." I grinned. Auntie had done it again. Perhaps Grandpa and Eng weren't out of luck yet. "I have a hunch you're going to talk to Carl again," I said.

"Gotcha." Auntie nodded.

Evie shook her head. "Chris said that you were smart. I didn't realize just how smart. He says you can fix any situation."

"I wouldn't pay much attention to him," Auntie said modestly.

I slapped Auntie's shoulder. "Are you kidding? She's the best. She's solved two cases that the police couldn't."

Evie looked really thoughtful as we walked to the prop room. Carl was kicking Leo when we peeked inside. "Come on. Work! Or I'm going to turn you into a footstool."

Maybe this was why they were shooting another scene.

Auntie stepped inside. "Carl, can we ask you one quick question?"

"Not now," Carl snapped. "I'm busy."

Auntie could be persistent. "We just want to know how you got your breakfast. Tell us and we won't bother you again."

"Some guy brought it," Carl said without looking up.

"Which guy?" Auntie asked, suddenly alert.

"Some guy in a catering jacket," Carl said. "I was too busy to look at faces."

As we left the trailer, I said to Auntie, "So maybe the dealer put on a caterer's jacket and took the box over to Carl."

"I'll help you ask the caterers," Evie volunteered.

We checked quickly with the caterers. None of them had taken the food to Carl, nor was there a jacket missing.

"They might not have noticed yet," Auntie said.

"Where are we going now?" I asked.

"To Errol's flower shop," Auntie said. "He sells firecrackers on the side. Nick must be one of Errol's rivals, so maybe he knows how to find him."

Errol was an old friend of Auntie's who had helped us on another case. We called him Uncle Errol.

"Where is the shop?" Evie asked curiously. "Is it very far away?"

I told her the Chinatown address, but she still didn't know where that was.

"I don't know Chinatown very well," she confessed. "My family doesn't like coming down here. We're northern Chinese, and the Chinatowners are from the south."

"You speak Mandarin, while they speak Cantonese," Auntie said.

Evie chuckled. "My parents learned some Cantonese. They found that when they went shopping in Chinatown, they got charged more if they spoke Mandarin."

I was shocked. "Cantonese wouldn't do that."

"To an outsider all Chinese might seem the same, but there are a lot of differences among the Chinese groups," Auntie explained. "There are a lot of other Chinese besides the ones you meet in Chinatown."

I was embarrassed to say that I thought Chinatown was the center of the Chinese world. "There are?"

"Sure," Auntie said. "It just so happens that most of the Chinese in Chinatown come from southern China, but

China's a big country. Deserts and mountains can isolate one area from another. And then there were a lot of civil wars, when one bunch was fighting another. That's why there are so many dialects."

"I never thought about that," I admitted.

"And that doesn't include all the Chinese who left China for other countries," Auntie added.

My head was feeling a little dizzy. "You mean they didn't all come to America?"

"No," Auntie explained. "Some went to Malaysia. Some went to Vietnam or Indonesia. Others went to Australia or the Philippines. There are whole bunches down in Peru and Cuba too. Jamaica. South Africa. Pick a spot on the globe and you'll find Chinese there."

"But why?" I asked.

"They needed to find work so they could send money home to China," Auntie said. "Things were that bad back there."

I got back to the point. "But we're really all Chinese. We shouldn't cheat one another."

"There are a lot of prejudices that can grow up over those differences," Auntie said. "There shouldn't be, but there are." She stopped abruptly. "But you don't want to hear an old lady wander on."

"What do you mean about prejudices? What sort of differences?" Evie asked.

Auntie shrugged. "Well, I got snubbed too." Auntie suddenly became shy. "That was too long ago—when dinosaurs roamed the Earth."

"Come on, Auntie," I coaxed.

"Please tell us," Evie begged.

Auntie scratched the tip of her nose. "Well, it was a little different back then. The immigration laws had made it hard for Chinese to come in, so there weren't that many of us, and we all pretty much came from the same background. Most of the kids from Chinatown went to the same elementary and junior high schools. Our family was really poor, so the other kids treated us like dirt."

I felt sorry for Auntie. "Because you couldn't match their clothes and stuff?"

Auntie shut her eyes as if she didn't like to remember those days. "I used to get beat up all the time. But then I found if I made them laugh, they liked me."

"Did Uncle Errol snub you too when you were kids?" I asked her.

"He made my life miserable," Auntie said with a laugh. I realized that laughing was her reaction to most anything. I guessed clowning had become her way of life.

She shrugged. "But so did a lot of my classmates."

I thought of how Chinatown acted about Auntie. "Well, they more than like you now, Auntie. They love you."

"Do you really think so, kiddo?" Auntie asked shyly. Even now, after all her successes, there was still that embarrassed little girl inside.

"I know so," I assured her.

"That could be the title for my tell-all autobiography: *Ugly Duckling Makes Good*," Auntie said.

"I don't know if I'll ever make it out of the Duckling stage. Television isn't what I thought it'd be," Evie confessed. "I was petrified when we were in that scene. And if I'd known Chris was going to get into trouble, I would never have done it."

Auntie patted her on the shoulder. "None of us has a crystal ball, kiddo."

Evie lifted her head determinedly. "Maybe not, but I'm going to do my best to make sure Chris stays out of trouble from now on."

Evie was definitely earning points.

e waited around for a half hour to make sure Chris was all right. Charley escorted my brother back. "Here's your Rocky."

Chris didn't look nearly as confident as when he had first gone off. "They told me not to leave the city."

"The cops are funny that way, when you punch a guy and make threats and then someone takes a shot at him," Charley said calmly, as if this happened all the time.

"But I explained that I wasn't making a threat to Clark," Chris said.

"No, it was to me," Evie insisted.

Charley eyed Evie. "So you're the third part of the triangle."

"There's no triangle," Chris snapped.

"That's what they all say, kid." Charley pulled a gold case from his suit pocket. I guessed he was a big-league hitter, just like Auntie had said. "Here's my card just in case. For Tiger Lil, I'll go anywhere anytime." Then he grinned at Auntie. "Well, gotta go, Tiger Lil. I got to get back to taking depositions. Only for you."

Auntie dimpled. "Give me a call and we'll set up dinner."

"It's going to cost you," Charley warned. "I know the menu at the Fleur de Lys by heart."

As Charley swaggered away, Chris studied the card. "Do you really think I'll need him anymore?"

"Just for insurance," Auntie said, "we're going to pay a visit to Uncle Errol's."

"It's a funny time to buy a bouquet," Chris said, putting Charley's card away.

"We're looking for information on the case," I said.

To my surprise, Chris didn't want any of us to go. "It's as much for you as for Auntie's client," I pointed out.

Chris tried to stand his ground. "Look. You lucked out the last two times, but in case you didn't notice, this time they're using real bullets. I couldn't stand it if something happened to you because of me."

Auntie chucked Chris under the chin. "Listen, kiddo. If I wouldn't listen to Bruce Lee and Clint Eastwood, what makes you think I'd listen to you?"

Chris looked embarrassed at having Auntie treat him like a kid. "They were using fake bullets."

"You try working in the Malaysian jungle on a shoot. They had mosquitoes this big." Auntie held her thumb and index finger three inches apart. "And I dodged every one of them."

Chris jerked his head toward me. "At least leave Lily out of this."

I latched onto Auntie's arm like a leech. "No way. I'm

her assistant. Besides, I can handle myself. I got street smarts."

Chris rolled his eyes. "You really believe that, don't you?"

That's the trouble with big brothers. They think they can boss you around even when you're better at something than they are. "How many cases have you solved?" I shot back.

He glowered at me and then grunted. "Since you're both determined to go, I guess I'd better go along too. I won't screw up the next time."

"Listen, kiddo," Auntie scolded him, "you leave dodging bullets to me."

Unfortunately, Evie decided that she was also going to be brave. "Then I'm going too," she announced.

"Oh, no," Chris said, shaking his head. "You're going home." For once, I agreed with my big brother.

Evie folded her arms. "I'll go crazy if I have to wait at home. I'll be imagining all the things that can happen to you. And I've got a good imagination."

Chris got a goofy grin. "You'd be worried about me?"

Evie shrugged. "A little."

As far as I was concerned, Evie would be a hundred-and-ten-pound anchor. I thought it was a fine time for her to get lovey-dovey, and I snorted in disgust.

"I really think you ought to stay behind, Evie," Auntie said.

Evie hooked a thumb behind the strap of her purse. "It's a free country, you know. I can follow you wherever I want."

Auntie's frown slowly turned to a smile. "I was just as single-minded as you are when I was your age. So come along, but you have to promise to run when I tell you to."

Evie held out a foot. "I'll kick off these shoes. Barefoot, I can outrun anyone."

As we passed by the laundry, Grandpa Eng said in Chinese, *"Tiger Lil, what's the news?"*

"Still working at it," Auntie said. She didn't tell him any more. I guess she didn't want to worry him.

"I should help you," Grandpa Eng said.

Auntie shook her head. *"I think it'd be better if you stayed behind."*

Grandpa Eng looked stubborn. *"When I first brought him to America, he wanted a toy for Christmas. And I promised him I'd buy it for him. But then I didn't have money."*

"He got mad?" I asked in Chinese. Maybe that helped explain why Eng was so angry at his grandfather.

"Very." The old man sighed. *"And I kept wanting to make him happy, so I kept making promises. I always wound up breaking them, but I'm not going to anymore."*

"We may have to move fast sometimes," Auntie said doubtfully.

Grandpa Eng looked determined. *"Don't worry about what happens to me. My grandson comes first."*

I felt sorry for Grandpa Eng. "Maybe he could act as our lookout," I suggested to Auntie.

Grandpa Eng looked at Chris, Evie, and me. *"Are all of you her assistants?"* He smiled at Auntie. *"You must be doing very well."*

"I beg your pardon," Evie said in English to Grandpa Eng. "I can only speak Mandarin, not Cantonese."

"Where you from?" Grandpa Eng asked, switching to English.

"Taiwan," Evie said.

It seemed funny that the only way two Chinese like Evie and Grandpa Eng could communicate was in English.

Auntie led us through Chinatown and into the alley where Uncle Errol's florist shop was. "You'd better wait out here," Auntie warned Evie and Grandpa Eng. "Errol might not talk in front of strangers. Lily and Chris are family."

As they waited in the alley, we headed inside. The tiny shop was so crowded with plants that there was only a narrow aisle through the greenery, and the warm, humid air made it really seem like a jungle.

Waiting at the end of the jungle was Uncle Errol. "Lil!" he said, grinning, his double chins wagging. Throwing down his racing form, he hugged Auntie and then greeted Chris and me. He'd met both of us at various banquets in Chinatown. He was a friend of our parents, and I'd spoken with him on our last case. Auntie chatted with him for a little while about old times. You would never have known that Auntie had been hurt by him when they were young.

After a while Auntie steered their conversation around to firecrackers. Uncle Errol shook his head. "I finally got out of that racket. It was getting too tough. All the gangs were wanting a slice of the pie."

"Would you know someone named Nick?" Auntie asked.

Uncle Errol swung his arms back and forth in a cross several times. "Steer clear of him. He's the reason I got out of the game. He started up a new gang in the Tenderloin. They're all Vietnamese Chinese. They were the ones who came in and sprayed Stockton with automatic guns."

I'd read about that. Nobody had gotten hurt, but windows and cars had gotten shot up. "Why did they do that, anyway?"

"They were trying to make a name for themselves and scare the other gangs. They wanted to cut in on the Chinatown territory for firecracker sales." Uncle Errol circled an index finger by his right temple. "But they're just out of control."

Auntie and I glanced at each other. If they were crazy enough to shoot up a street with guns, then maybe they were up to killing Clark Tom.

"Do you think he's wild enough to frame Eng for murder?" Auntie asked.

"Eng the gang leader?" Uncle Errol frowned. "You got to hang around with a better crowd, Tiger Lil. First Nick. Now Eng."

"I'll try, but what about my question?" Auntie insisted.

"It'd be more like Nick to put a bullet in Eng himself," Uncle Errol said. "He'd want the satisfaction of doing it himself."

"But could Nick let the cops do the dirty work for him?" Auntie asked.

Uncle Errol rubbed his jaw. "Well, he'd like the idea of fooling the cops. I guess so."

"Where can we find him, Errol?" Auntie asked.

"The Tenderloin isn't for Chinatowners," Errol argued.

Auntie leaned on the counter. "But do you have an address? It's important, Errol." And she told him about what had happened that morning. "I'm doing this for Eng's grandfather," she finished.

"You can't fix the whole world," Uncle Errol cautioned.

"I can try," Auntie insisted.

Uncle Errol dug a phone book out from beneath the counter. "I heard he used to hang out at the Hue Sandwich Shop. You could call the place and see if he was in."

I didn't recognize the name. "Hue? Is that a Chinese city?" I whispered to Chris.

"No, it's a city in Vietnam," Chris told me.

Auntie swung the book around to see the address. "I think I'll just go over. I don't want him skipping out."

Uncle Errol looked troubled. "I thought you were going to just talk to him on the phone. If I'd known you were going to do that, I'd never have told you."

Auntie patted his cheek to comfort him. "I'll be okay, Errol. I can still run pretty fast."

"At least leave the kids behind," Uncle Errol said, nodding to us.

Auntie rubbed her chin. "Yeah, maybe you're right."

"Not a chance," I said. "We can run even faster than Auntie."

Chris looked even more serious than usual. "I won't let anything happen to them."

"Forget it, kiddos," Auntie said. "This time I fly solo."

When we stepped outside the shop, Auntie told Evie

and Grandpa Eng, "You go back to the set. I've got an errand to run, but I'll be back."

"But Auntie—" I began to protest.

Auntie wagged a finger at me. "You heard me." Her face put on a stern expression that I had never seen before. So I didn't even try to argue.

Chris waited until Auntie had stepped out of the alley. "You go home."

I guess it was still eating at him that he hadn't done anything to help prevent the shooting.

"Auntie didn't want us along," I said.

"She's going to need help," Chris said.

"Then I'm going too," I said.

"It's dangerous, twerp," Chris snapped.

I planted a fist on my hip. "Oh, yeah? How many cases have you solved? I've handled two. You're just an amateur compared to me."

"You go, I go," Grandpa Eng said.

"Count me in," Evie said.

We hung back behind Auntie and waited until the last moment to board the bus. It was so jammed, she never saw us.

We had to transfer to another bus. Again, we got off at the last second at the tail end of the huge crowd that flooded off the bus at Market Street.

Fortunately there were two buses, one behind the other, heading to the Tenderloin. So we let Auntie take the first and got on the second.

The clouds still hung over the Tenderloin too. It was a part of San Francisco that I had never been in, and I don't think my parents would have wanted me to walk through it. We passed by rows of massage parlors and other sleazy places that sandwiched little run-down hotels. Looking through the bus window, I could see elderly people sitting in the lobby and watching the traffic.

"How can they stay in a neighborhood like this?" I asked Chris.

Grandpa Eng spoke first. "I got friend. He live this neighborhood. He retired. This place all he can afford. Chinatown rents too high. Other old people maybe just like him."

Chris sympathized. "It can't be an easy life for them. There are a lot of junkies in this area who would be happy to mug them for a few dollars. Even buying groceries could be a real hassle."

"Poor people," I said.

Grandpa Eng nodded his head. "That why I still work at laundry twelve hours. Do all lousy jobs there. Sleep on dirty laundry."

"That's awful," Chris said. "You should quit."

Grandpa shrugged. "Who hire old man like me? And boss, he give me few bucks every week for bus fare."

"But you just said you live in Chinatown," Chris said. "Why do you need bus fare to commute?"

Grandpa Eng stared at him as if he had just landed from a flying saucer.

"Another word for salary," Grandpa explained to Chris. For someone who talked about helping the downtrodden masses, it seemed like Chris didn't know them very well.

I hadn't known what "bus fare" meant either, so I

was glad Chris had asked. Even though I had grown up in Chinatown, there was still a lot of stuff I didn't know about the old-timers. I'd gotten similar stares from other old-timers just like Grandpa Eng—some of whom were too polite to tell me how stupid they thought I was.

"Oh," Chris said in a small, embarrassed voice. "I bet the amount's so little, you couldn't even call it a salary."

Grandpa Eng didn't contradict Chris. Instead, he stared through the bus window and shuddered. "I not want leave Chinatown for this." It was plain that the Tenderloin would be exile for him.

"Maybe Auntie can help you find another job somehow," I suggested.

"*I'm too old,*" he said, shaking his head miserably. "*And even if she could get me a job, where could I live on what they'd pay?*"

I had faith in Auntie, though. "Auntie's good at fixing things," I assured him.

Evie pointed out the window. "She's gotten off."

We had to get off at the next stop. I thought Grandpa Eng might have trouble, but he moved in small, balanced steps. When the bus pulled over to the curb, I shoved the doors open and stepped onto the sidewalk. I moved aside quickly so the others could follow me. Chris brought up the rear, acting as a shield so the other passengers couldn't knock our group over.

As we walked along, Chris turned his head from left to right, staring. "It's like Chinatown."

He was right. There were a lot of little restaurants, groceries, and even a few bookshops. A music store was playing Chinese-sounding music over loudspeakers, but I didn't recognize the words.

"Is that a different Chinese dialect?" I asked Grandpa Eng.

Grandpa Eng leaned his head to the side, listening. "I think it Vietnamese."

I glanced up at the nearest store sign. The writing looked sort of like Chinese characters, but not quite. "So is that Vietnamese too?" I asked.

"I think so," Chris said. The dolls and other items in the store window looked Asian, but they weren't the same as the ones in Chinatown. The grocery store had some things we could have found in Chinatown, but there were also a lot of things I had never seen before. When I looked through the restaurant windows, I didn't recognize a lot of the food, either.

Except for the language, though, I felt like the crowded sidewalks could have been a family scene in Chinatown. Elderly grannies and grandpas stood gossiping with one another. Mothers with babies strapped to their backs, and holding plastic shopping bags bulging with food, hurried by. There were kids playing on the sidewalk too.

"It's just like Chinatown," Chris said. "A lot of decent families trying to make a living."

I was beginning to feel more comfortable. "Just like home."

We passed by a café called the Saigon Gardens. When I looked at the menu taped to the window, I saw the same kind of food I always ate in Chinatown. And when I glanced inside, I saw familiar food on the plates.

That only confused me more. "How can they call this the Saigon Gardens when it's got Chinatown food?" I knew from history class that Saigon was in Vietnam.

"There are a lot of Chinese who went to Vietnam, too," Chris said. "My Jewish friends talk about the Diaspora that spread the Jewish people all over the world—even to China. But there was a Chinese one as well. Life was so hard in China that they had to leave to survive."

"Chinese really can adapt," I said.

All my life, I had thought the Chinese were Chinatown. I was beginning to realize they were all over the world. There was Evie from Taiwan, and now this.

I should have remembered that there's a bad guy for every thousand good ones on the globe.

CHAPTER NINE

Chris pointed to a sign. "There's the Hue."

It looked like any cheap little café. It had blue and black tiles beneath the window. The concrete sides had been painted, but the old lettering showed through: THE BIJOU CAFÉ.

Looking through the window, we could see a narrow room with a counter on one side and Formica-covered tables and chairs on the other. Behind the counter were a cash register and a couple of tall urns—I guessed they were for coffee and hot water. There were a few cakes behind the window under the counter. Each was topped with a bright red cherry.

At the cash register was an Asian girl who looked about Evie's age. She had short hair and wore bright lipstick like one of those stars from the silent movies. She watched us as we came in, and so did a half dozen boys who were lounging by a pay phone on the wall. The boys were all dressed alike, with pointy black shoes, tight black pants, short jackets, and skinny ties. Their hair was long, and each had a strand of hair braided over the left temple. At the end of the braid each wore a colored bead. One had a red bead, one a blue. The others had white.

I figured they were gang members. So the neighborhood was like Chinatown in this too. There were a lot of hardworking, decent families as well as a few bad people.

Auntie was standing with her back to the window, talking with the girl at the counter, when the boy with the red bead noticed us peering through the window. At his gesture, several white beads leaped up and headed for us.

"Uh-oh," I said. "Better keep going."

We started to hurry on when the door jerked open. "What do you want?" one of the white beads demanded.

I rubbed my stomach nervously. "We were just looking for a snack, but I think we're going on."

However, the commotion had made Auntie turn around. She gave a start when she saw us. Red Bead must have been keeping an eye on her as well, because he called through the open door, "Bring them inside."

I tried to stroll inside, looking as cool and nonchalant as I could. "Why, Auntie. Imagine meeting you here."

Auntie glared. "I told you to leave this to me."

"What do you want?" Red Bead asked.

Auntie turned to him, trying to sound cheerful. "We're looking for a fellow called Nick."

"Why?" Red Bead called.

"We have some questions to ask," Auntie explained politely. "Are you Nick?"

Red Bead touched the decoration in his hair. "Does this look yellow?"

"I didn't realize the yellow was Nick's color," Auntie said.

Maybe the colored beads were like insignia in the army, I thought.

Red Bead slouched against the wall, his head just beneath the pay phone. "So why do you want Nick?"

Auntie seemed very calm despite everything, but then she was a good actor. "We hoped to talk to him about some firecrackers."

"If you need firecrackers, you can talk to me," Red Bead said. "The name's Ivan. I'm Nick's second-in-command."

"Well, Ivan, I don't actually want firecrackers. I want to ask him about an earlier . . . uh . . . transaction," Auntie said carefully. "I think Nick tried to sell some firecrackers to a television show."

Ivan's eyes narrowed. "How do you know about that? Are you from the show?"

"No, but there's an acquaintance who's in a little trouble. So we just needed to ask Nick some questions," Auntie said.

Ivan wound the telephone receiver's cable around his fingers. "What do you know about Nick?"

"Nothing, really," Auntie said quickly.

Blue Bead, though, leaned forward and squinted at Auntie. "I know you."

Ivan let the receiver cable uncoil like a snake. "Maybe because she's a cop."

I froze, but to my relief, Blue Bead shook his head. "No. That's not it." He wagged his index finger like a metronome on its side. "But where was it?"

"I've made a few movies," Auntie said modestly. "Maybe you saw the one I did with Bruce Lee?"

By now I was used to having people recognize Auntie, but Chris and Evie weren't. Chris looked surprised that Blue Bead would know her. Evie shot a look at Auntie as if she were having to do a quick reevaluation of her.

"No, no. You were with someone bigger," Blue Bead said.

"Bigger than Bruce Lee?" Auntie asked, puzzled.

Suddenly Blue Bead spread his arms out high and wide. "I know. You were with Gamera, the giant turtle." He spun around in a circle. "He spins around when fire comes out of his backside. That was my favorite Japanese monster movie. We used to see them dubbed in Vietnam."

"What came out of her backside?" Ivan asked sarcastically.

I knew who Gamera was, but I hadn't realized Auntie had been in one of those. Auntie didn't always mention all of the films she had been in.

"You were in a monster film?" Chris asked her.

Blue Bead nodded so that his decoration shook. "They showed it with Chinese subtitles."

Auntie looked embarrassed. "I did it for a lark, kiddo."

From past conversations, I knew even a famous star like Auntie had her ups and downs. Maybe she had done it for fun. Maybe she had done it to pay her bills. Whatever the reason, the gang looked impressed.

Blue Bead snatched a napkin from a holder on a table. "Can I have your autograph?"

"Me too," said a boy with a white bead. He got his own

napkin as the others snatched napkins out of other holders.

As nervous as Auntie was, she couldn't disappoint her fans—even dangerous ones. While she signed the napkins, Chris folded his arms thoughtfully.

"Does this happen often?" he asked me.

"All the time," I bragged. "You might not think much of movies, but they have a big impact. Lots of strangers think of Auntie as a friend."

"She really is famous," Chris muttered, as if he hadn't believed it before.

"You should be proud," Grandpa Eng scolded Chris. "Your auntie big, big star."

However, if I had hoped the gang might let us go because Auntie was such a big celebrity, I was mistaken.

When Auntie was done, she put away her pen. "Well, since Nick's not here, I guess I'll come back later."

Ivan reached a hand up and lifted the receiver from its cradle. "Nick decided to take a little . . . vacation. He's worked so hard lately, teaching our competitors a lesson."

One of the boys snickered. "We showed those Powell Street Boys."

Ivan shot him a warning look.

I wondered if that had anything to do with the shooting on Stockton Street. If I'd masterminded that, I'd be hiding out from the cops too.

"Nick would hate to miss you. Why don't I give him a call?" Ivan asked.

"No, don't bother him," Auntie said, motioning for us to head for the door. She was nervous.

"No, no trouble. Maybe he wants an autograph too."
Ivan snapped his fingers, and Blue Bead handed him some
coins. Twisting around in his seat, Ivan put the coins in
and began to punch the buttons.

Auntie glanced at her watch. "Oh, my, look at the
time. I've really got to run. Give Nick my regrets."

"We wouldn't think of letting you go." Ivan nodded to
the boys. Even though they were still in awe of Auntie, the
boys moved to stand between the tables to block our exit.

"Stick near me," Chris warned Evie and me in a whisper. Evie pressed close to him, but I stayed where I was. He
might think he was Superman, but I knew better.

"It's ringing," Ivan said out loud to no one in particu-
lar. "Hello, Nick. Yeah, it's Ivan. We got a woman here
who wants to talk to you. They say she's a famous film star.
Made monster movies in Japan." He grinned. "No, she
wasn't the monster—I think."

Even now Auntie couldn't help objecting. "But I got
top billing, and my name was in a box."

Ivan just raised his eyebrows mockingly. "Uh-huh. Uh-
huh." He sniffed the air noisily. "I smell the cops too,
Nick."

Auntie waved a hand between us and herself. "Do we
look like cops?"

Ivan said something in a low voice into the telephone,
listened for a moment, and then said to Auntie, "Nick
wants to know who told you about the firecrackers. He's
pretty fussy who he deals with. He says there's cops everywhere."

"A guy at the TV show told me," Auntie said.

Ivan gave a snort and relayed the information to Nick. After a moment, he asked, "Or did some cop? Nick wants to know if you're working for them."

"What would a big star be doing working for the cops?" Blue Bead asked.

"What would a big star want with Nick?" Ivan countered.

Auntie was a great actor, but she wasn't so good at ad-libbing. "Well, when friends open up stores and restaurants in Chinatown, we need lots and lots of firecrackers. I heard you can provide them cheaper than your rivals."

Ivan listened to Nick for a moment and then smirked. "Nick says to check them for a wire."

From the cop shows, I knew he wanted to see if we were wired either for a tape recorder or for a mike, to transmit the conversation to the cops.

Two boys started forward. Chris balled his hands into fists, but Auntie shook her head.

"It's okay," Evie reassured him.

It wasn't okay with me, but I didn't see what choice I had.

The boys searched us efficiently. They even went through each of the autograph books, though I don't think they recognized Clark's scrawl or they might have confiscated them. When they were done, they said something in Vietnamese to Ivan.

"Well, now that we've cleared up that mystery, we've really got to go," Auntie said. Turning, I tried to push through the boys, but the boys pushed back.

Ivan said something into the phone and then nodded

his head. "I got you, Nick." He hung up the receiver. "Nick says to wait until he can think about this."

Auntie fluttered her hand. "All right. I'll call later. What's the number on that phone?" She really sounded nervous.

Nick laced his fingers together. "Now that you're here, I think you're going to stay."

"You run," Grandpa Eng said, and raised his hands in a martial arts pose.

Chris slid in beside him. "Yeah."

Auntie grabbed Grandpa Eng's arm before he could take a swing at the gang members blocking our way. "You can't help your grandson that way." Auntie used her hip to nudge Chris out of his pose. "And quit trying to impress Evie. Just run. "

I had a lot of practice getting past Chris. He used to like to tease me by blocking my path. Lowering my shoulder, I rammed into a white bead. "Out of my way." He went tumbling backward into a table.

Out of the corner of my eye, I saw another boy falling to the floor, and then Evie was almost a blur heading for the door. One of the boys was down on the ground—I suppose Evie had knocked him down. She was more athletic than she looked.

In the meantime, Auntie was flailing around with her big purse. "I learned a thing or two from Gamera, kiddos."

"Stop where you are," Ivan barked, "or the old man gets it."

I turned to see Grandpa Eng on the floor with Ivan sitting on top of him. With one hand Ivan held Grandpa

Eng's head up by his hair. With his other hand he held a knife against Grandpa Eng's throat.

I froze. Auntie lowered her purse. The next instant Evie was crying out in alarm, "Don't you touch me."

Blue Bead was pulling her away from the front door.

"Let go of her." Chris headed to the rescue.

Auntie stuck her foot out and tripped him neatly so that he fell face forward. "Sorry, kiddo, but it's no time for heroics."

Shoving Evie toward us, Blue Bead turned to the door and locked it with a quick twist of his wrist.

I thought about calling to the girl behind the counter, but she had already ducked for cover. I looked through the glass and saw her squatting down behind the desserts. I suspected she had a lot of practice getting out of the gang's way.

"You should be ashame," Grandpa Eng scolded Ivan.

"You should be ashame," Ivan mimicked him with a sneer.

When he stood up, I could see that he wasn't much taller than me. "I think you're going to be very sorry the next time I talk to Nick." He jerked his head toward a door at the back of the shop. "Lock them up."

CHAPTER TEN

After they locked us in the storage room, Grandpa Eng slumped sadly in a corner. "They just like grandson."

"Why did you trip me?" Chris asked Auntie angrily.

Auntie stuck her face almost nose-to-nose with his. "This is a time for brains, not brawn."

"You're trying to act just like a hero in one of those television shows you hate so much," I snapped.

Chris' shoulders sagged. "I'm not a wimp either," he said lamely, glancing at Evie. I guessed he was still trying to impress her.

"You can save that for later." Auntie began to rummage around in her coat pockets. "What have you got, kiddos? Anything to pick a lock?"

I had seen Auntie in action before, and I began to search my own pockets. "All I've got is this." I held up a handkerchief and the yellow gum wrapper and foil that I had picked up when Evie had discarded them.

After a moment Evie began to go through her own

pockets, and a few seconds later a still resentful Chris copied her.

Auntie held up her empty hands in disgust. "Not even a paper clip."

"I got some change," Grandpa Eng said.

"Kleenex," Chris said, "and Charley Moy's business card."

Evie smiled apologetically. "I wish they hadn't taken my purse. I had stuff in there that you could have used." They had taken Auntie's too.

"No hairpins?" Auntie asked, looking at Evie and me. When we shook our heads, she sighed. "Well, I wouldn't have known how to pick a lock anyway," she finally admitted.

Looking annoyed, Chris slapped his sides. "Well, what was the point then?"

"The point is that you don't give up," Auntie snapped, and she held out her hand. "Give me those gum wrappers. Maybe if I fold them, I can make them stiffer. And then we can try to pick the lock."

I handed over both the paper and the foil.

We watched her hopefully as she folded them over and over until they were almost the size and shape of a bobby pin. Hunkering down in front of the lock, she stuck out her tongue as she tried to pick it, but her improvised tool kept bending. Finally she put it away in her pocket. "Nope. We're going to have to get out with something else."

I was ready to try to cheer her up, but Auntie wasn't discouraged in the least. Instead, she began to check the room.

In her Tiger Lil movies—the films that had made her famous—she had been tough and resourceful. The more I learned about Auntie, the more I had realized she wasn't just acting. That was just the way she was.

I think Chris was beginning to understand that too. "So what's next?" he asked her.

"Let's each take one part of the room," Evie suggested, sounding hopeful all of a sudden.

Grandpa Eng took heart as well. "I'll be the lookout at the door."

We hunted around the room for something useful, but it was just filled with stacks of sacks of flour and sugar and huge cans of baking powder. Metal shelves lined another wall with large cans of lard. Against the next wall was a metal sink.

One by one, we had to admit we had come up with nothing. I was the last next to Auntie.

"It's not exactly the Fairmont, is it?" I said, plopping down on a stack of sugar sacks—enough to rot even Godzilla's teeth. The sacks were awfully lumpy, though, so I squirmed around, trying to find a comfortable position.

Even then, Auntie refused to be discouraged. "But the room service ought to be great—all the cakes you can eat," she cracked. However, her eyes roamed around the room as if she were looking for some other method of escape.

Chris crossed his legs. "How can you make jokes when we're in such a tight scrape?"

Auntie checked out the small window, but it had bars. "I don't know, kiddo. I guess I was born telling a knock-knock joke to the doctor."

As far as I could tell, the only way out was the door we had come through.

"Don't you ever get tired of making smart remarks?" Chris wondered.

"No, it's just as natural as breathing."

I thought about what she had told Evie and me. "I guess you've been doing it since you were a kid."

Auntie scratched the back of her neck. She was always so calm and confident that it was odd to see her uncomfortable. "Can we change the topic?"

I leaned close to Auntie so the others couldn't overhear. "You know I'll never make fun of you, Auntie," I whispered.

Auntie let her hand drop. "I know, kiddo." She gave me a quick hug.

At that moment, one of the gang opened the door, and the girl from behind the counter entered. She had a small tray with five Styrofoam cups and five small cakes. "I thought you might like some tea and snacks," she said as the guard closed the door again.

"Thanks," I said. The tea was nice and hot, and the cakes were chock-full of cream and chocolate icing.

Auntie took her share with the rest of us. "Yes, thank you . . ."

"Marie," the girl said.

"Thank you, Marie," Auntie said. "I'm Lil, and that's Lily." She gestured toward me with the cup.

"Yes, Miss Leung," Marie gushed. "I saw your movies back home in Vietnam. You're my favorite star."

"Which ones?" Auntie asked.

"*Feet of Fury* and *Killer Granny*. They were subtitled in Vietnamese," Marie said. Setting down her tray, she excitedly took out an order pad and a pen. "Could I have your autograph?"

It seemed like Auntie's films had reached wherever Asians were.

"Sure," Auntie said, "anything for a fan." As she wrote slowly, she pretended to have another idea. "Do you like Clark Tom?"

Marie straightened and her eyes widened with excitement. "Oh, yes," she gushed. "He's my favorite. I watch his show every chance I get."

Auntie went on writing. "I thought I was your favorite," she teased.

Marie made a quick correction. "You're my favorite female star. He's my favorite male."

"Well, I promised to bring a special gift to Clark, but obviously I can't do that now. So will you call Clark? Tell him that Errol will know where the package is. I wrote down Errol's address." Auntie handed back the pad.

It took a moment for Marie to recover her breath. "Me? Talk to Clark Tom?"

Auntie capped the pen and held it out. "Maybe he'll even give you an autographed picture."

Marie took the pen and tucked it into a pocket. "I don't think I can use the phone outside. I might have to wait till this evening, when I get off."

"I don't think it can wait that long," Auntie said.

"I can't leave before then or they'll get suspicious," Marie said.

When she left, I whispered to Auntie, "Do you think she'll make the phone call?"

Evie began to eat daintily. "She'd walk across a burning desert to speak to Clark."

Chris eyed her speculatively. "Would you?"

"Don't be silly," Evie said. "I have some self-respect."

"I did dumber things when I was her age and had a crush," Auntie admitted.

"I'll never do that," I snorted.

Grandpa Eng chuckled knowingly. "You too young."

"Give yourself a few more years," Auntie advised.

I tried to change the subject. "Do you really think the call can't wait till this evening?"

"I'm not sure, kiddo," Auntie said, but from the way she gobbled down her cake, I knew she was nervous. I'd lost my appetite, so I offered her mine.

"No, thanks, kiddo." She suddenly looked thoughtful.

"What's up?" I asked.

She put her hands in her pockets and took out the folded foil and paper. Carefully she unfolded them and separated the two.

"Have you got an idea?" Chris asked eagerly. Grandpa Eng and Evie had both perked up as well.

Before Auntie could answer, the door started to open. Hastily Auntie put the paper and foil into her pocket as Ivan strolled in. Closing the door, he leaned against it. "I just spoke to Nick. He's still thinking about what to do with you."

Auntie kept her hands in her coat pockets. "I hope he doesn't think of the obvious."

Ivan went over and sat on some flour sacks. "Nick hates to do the expected. He's always got a lot of new ideas. That's what gave him the yellow bead over me."

From the corner of my eye, I saw Chris tensing. Despite what Auntie had told him, he still wanted to use brawn. Fortunately, Evie grabbed hold of his arm to keep him from doing anything stupid.

"If the yellow bead is the sign of the boss, what's the red bead mean?" Auntie pointed to his braid.

Ivan fingered his own bead. "This is the badge of the second-in-command."

I could see that Auntie was wriggling her hand inside her pocket. What was she up to?

"Is Nick imaginative about revenge?" she asked.

Ivan shivered. "That's when he's at his best."

"So he was behind the shooting on the set?" Auntie asked. Her hand was still squirming in her pocket like a puppy.

Ivan folded his arms. "What shooting?"

"He framed Eng by sneaking real bullets into a prop gun," Auntie explained.

Ivan pursed his lips. "I heard about Eng getting arrested, but I never heard the details."

"He didn't tell you his plan?"

"I never know what Nick's thinking," Ivan said. "He keeps us all off-balance. Keeps shaking things up. Keeps moving around, you know? That's how he's survived."

"Well, it's a neat bit of revenge," Auntie agreed. "He gets even not only with Eng but with the show for backing off on the deal."

"Everyone says how smart Nick is," Ivan said smugly.

"I'd almost say you were jealous," Auntie observed.

"How would you feel if you always came in second?" Ivan asked. He got up abruptly. "But I know my place."

"You seem like too smart a fellow to be second-in-command for the rest of your life," Auntie said. "You'll be on top soon."

"I'd rather let Nick make all the hard decisions," Ivan said. "Which reminds me. I'd better report back to him."

He thought us so harmless that he turned his back on Auntie when he opened the door.

For all of her size, Auntie can move a lot faster than people realize. She was on him before he knew it, and she shoved him sprawling onto the floor. "He killed Nick," she shouted to the guard. From her coat pocket, she took out a small yellow ball. "I found this bead on the floor of the storage room."

Ivan jumped to his feet. "You're crazy. I just talked to Nick."

Auntie pocketed the ball. "You were just pretending to." She turned to the rest of the gang by the door. "Has anyone else ever talked to Nick?"

Ivan snarled, "She's lying. Lock her back up."

However, the gang members were busy looking at one another.

Auntie pursued her opportunity. "Has Nick ever called here himself, or is it always Ivan who phones him?"

The gang didn't say anything, but the they all stared at Ivan. It must have been just him.

"I order you to lock them up," Ivan yelled.

Auntie kept on pushing. "When did Nick take his 'vacation'? Was it before the shooting on Stockton?"

"It was after," Blue Bead said, folding his arms.

"Stop talking to her," Ivan snapped.

Auntie spoke quickly. "Did anyone actually hear Nick give the command to do it? Or did it come through Ivan?"

"The orders came from Ivan," Blue Bead said, looking thoughtful.

Ivan was almost quivering with rage. "Don't tell her anything, or Nick's going to be mad."

"And when did Nick go on vacation?" Auntie asked.

"Five days ago," Blue Bead said. I thought he could see where Auntie was heading.

"When I call Nick, you're going to be sorry," Ivan said threateningly.

Auntie spread her hands. "Go ahead. But this time maybe someone else should talk to him. Then you can ask if he really ordered you to put real bullets in the gun."

Ivan dropped his hand. "No, I can't get my friends in trouble with Nick. He only wants to talk to me. Just lock her up and we'll forget this happened."

Blue Bead jerked his head at Ivan. "I'll risk it. Call Nick."

Ivan jammed his thumb against his chest. "Don't you tell me what to do. Nick left me in charge."

"Then why was there a yellow bead in the storage room?" Auntie demanded.

Ivan looked nervous. "He must have lost it in here."

The gang gathered around Blue Bead. "I think you better call Nick now," Blue Bead said.

Suddenly Ivan bolted for the door, but one of the white beads tripped him so that he fell on his face. The next moment the gang was swarming all over him.

"What happened to Nick?" Blue Bead demanded.

"I don't know," Ivan said, and then he winced as someone twisted his arm. "Ow."

"He's dead, isn't he?" Blue Bead said. "It's just like she said. You killed him."

"Ow, ow. Yes," Ivan confessed. "I had to. That wimp was mad at me for the shooting. If it was up to him, we'd always be stuck in the Tenderloin. But if you listen to me, we'll own Chinatown. I got lots of ideas. Big ideas."

Blue Bead nodded toward us. "Put him in the storage room with them."

"Hey," I yelped, "we just helped you catch him for Nick's murder."

"You've done us a big favor," Blue Bead said, grinning, "so when we dispose of you, we'll make it quick and as painless as we can." He glared at Ivan. "Not like the way he'll end."

"Who says?" a white bead demanded.

"You want to take it easy on that thing?" Another white bead pointed at Ivan.

"No, but it's a question of the method," Blue Bead said. "That should be up to the new boss."

"Yeah, we need to pick a new one," a third white bead said.

"Okay, okay," Blue Bead said. "Lock them all up." When he glanced around, the others nodded.

Auntie jerked her head at Ivan. "You can't put us in with him."

"The closet?" Blue Bead asked, and again there was unanimous agreement.

"See if we ever help you out again," I muttered.

Unfortunately, it looked as if it would be the last thing we would get to do.

CHAPTER ELEVEN

Through the storage room door, I could hear the gang holding its election—if you could call it that. Everyone was shouting at the same time. Maybe the last one to get hoarse would win.

I turned to Auntie. "How did you know Nick was dead?"

She went over to the pile of flour sacks and sat down. "I didn't. I figured if I confused the situation, I could buy more time so Marie could call Clark."

Chris shook his head in admiration. "So it was a bluff."

"You don't want to play poker with Auntie," I advised him. I knew. I'd tried with some of my friends. We'd wound up losing our allowances. Of course, Auntie had then blown all her winnings on pizza for everyone.

"What was the yellow bead then?" Chris asked.

Auntie took out the yellow ball. It was the wadded-up gum wrapper. "Who says recycling is a waste of time?"

I went back to my original seat on the sugar sacks. "So I guess we just wait and hope Clark can bring the police."

Auntie pulled back each sleeve elaborately. "One more miracle coming up."

As Grandpa Eng sat down, he began to ball his fingers into a fist and then spread them again.

"Is there something wrong?" I asked him.

"Just old age," Grandpa Eng said. "I got roo-mah-tism in hands," he said, and he held up fingers like red claws.

"It probably doesn't help to handle boiling water so much in the laundry," Auntie said sympathetically.

"Got lot pains." He pointed at his knee. "I got ar-thri-tis there."

"That's not fair," Chris said, growing indignant. "You've worked hard all your life. You deserve more than this."

"I always too busy working. No time for my grandson," Grandpa Eng confessed. "But I sorry now."

"You couldn't help it," Auntie tried to assure him.

Grandpa Eng sat still for a moment, and then his shoulders sagged. "No, why lie? I lie all my life. I work hard when I got job, but I . . . I like whiskey too much. And whiskey, it like me. So I keep losing jobs as soon as I get."

"Is that why you never had any money to keep your promises to your grandson?" Chris asked.

Grandpa Eng cradled his head in his hands. "Some-times I drank up that money. I . . . marry before leave China and come America. I tell my wife I be home in three years. But that in 1933. I never keep that promise either."

"Never?" I asked, amazed.

He shook his head. "First, Japanese invade China. That in 1936. Then Communist take over. I try send money home every month, though," he said defensively.

"You couldn't have been making much yourself," Chris sympathized.

"No, I lie, I lie. I break that promise too," Grandpa Eng moaned miserably.

"But people have come over since then from China," I said. In fact, there were several dozen in my school.

"By then, my wife and son dead. There only my grandson," he said miserably. "So I beg and borrow. Then I bring him over." He shrugged. "I should have left him there."

Chris leaned forward. "It must've been pretty lonely being away from your family."

"Maybe drinking start that way. But no excuse." When he raised his head, we could see he had been crying. "Once my grandson here, I should stop, but I cannot. So when I home, I drunk. All my grandson know about me. I only stop when no money. So I get another job." He swung his arm in a slow circle. "Then whole thing start over. Gang more family to him than me."

We were all silent for a while, feeling sorry for the old man. Chris let out his breath in a rush. "It's one thing to read about this stuff in books. It's another to hear about it in person."

"Pretty strong stuff," Auntie said.

"It makes me realize just how much I don't know," Chris admitted. Getting up, he went over to Grandpa Eng. "Here's a tissue."

"I stupid, stupid old man," Grandpa Eng said, wiping his eyes on his sleeve. "Stupid, stupid, stupid."

Chris cleared his throat. "Things are going to be okay."

"He in jail. I in here," Grandpa Eng said miserably.

Chris glanced at Auntie. "But we've got my auntie. She almost got us out last time." He grinned at Auntie. "She's not really that good an actor, you know."

"Hey," I objected.

Chris went on. "You didn't let me finish. Auntie doesn't play a hero. She *is* a hero."

One good thing had come out of all this: Chris had come to a new respect for Auntie.

"And for my next trick . . . well, let's see." Auntie scratched her head.

All this time I had been squirming around, trying to find a more comfortable position. Finally, though, I gave up and got on my feet. "This is too much," I said in exasperation.

"Restless, kiddo?" Auntie asked sympathetically.

"I don't see how they use this sugar in baking. It's got a lot of lumps," I said, moving over to another stack, but it wasn't any better than the first.

"The cakes we ate turned out okay, though." Auntie got off her bag and went over to examine the first stack, poking and prodding. "This says GRANULATED SUGAR, but it's got as many corners as big sugar cubes."

Auntie began to pull at one corner until the paper tore. "And I wouldn't use it except in exploding cakes." She started to widen the hole.

I saw the familiar red packages of firecrackers. "This is where they're hiding their stock." I looked around, wondering how many more of the sugar sacks contained explosives.

Auntie wormed a package out. "There must be enough here to blow up the building."

CHAPTER TWELVE

Grandpa Eng, Chris, and Evie had all jumped off their stacks, but theirs turned out to be real food.

Auntie looked from the window at some cans on the shelf. "Hmm; that just might work."

I watched her as she picked up a can of lard. "What's the new miracle?"

"This isn't a miracle. This is science in action." Auntie took her coat off and held it up against the window. "This should muffle the sound," she said, and brought the can down against the glass.

It broke more loudly than any of us expected, and I stood there holding my breath as I waited for the gang to investigate the strange noise.

Grandpa Eng had gone over to listen at the door. "They still argue. Everyone want be boss."

"Are you trying to make a weapon?" Evie asked uncertainly.

"Not exactly." Auntie began searching around the room. "Find bits of dry paper. Tear up the sacks if you have to. And put it on the windowsill."

The rest of us scurried around. I didn't think anybody had ever bothered to clean up the storage room. In no time we had a small pile there.

Then Auntie held up a piece of the window glass so that the sun could shine through it, creating a small, bright dot on a piece of paper.

Chris looked shocked. "Auntie, you can't start a fire in here."

"Relax, kiddo. I'm not going to get anywhere near the firecrackers. We just want to make the boys think there's a fire in here. We're going to create a lot of smoke and maybe set off a string or two." She chuckled. "Old Carl would be proud of our special effects."

However, after about an hour, Auntie stifled a yawn. "Gee, it always works fast in the television shows."

I remembered one of them. "Maybe it works faster with a magnifying glass," I said. "Or maybe we can rub two sticks together."

Chris rubbed his chin. "I wish I'd paid more attention in physics."

Auntie used her free hand to massage the wrist that was holding the glass. "I tried sticks one time when I was making a Western. Clint bet me I couldn't do it. You have to be able to make the sticks move almost as fast a drill. If I had the kind of muscles that would let me do that, I could have punched out the whole gang."

"There goes another illusion." I sighed.

Auntie shifted the glass to her other hand. "Then I

won't tell you that Gamera isn't real."

I pretended to be shocked. "He isn't?"

Auntie leaned her chin against her free hand. "Naw, it's an actor in a rubber suit."

"But I bet it's a real tall actor," I insisted.

Auntie chuckled. "Getting bored, kiddo? Why don't you start piling more paper in that old can over there?"

"Let me help," Evie said, going over.

Grandpa Eng was still at the door. "Everything still okay."

The can was a couple of feet high and at least that wide. At one time it had held massive amounts of baking soda.

Chris had gone over too. "It's already full of trash," he said.

"We have to get rid of everything that won't burn," I said, beginning to toss out nonburnables.

Auntie looked up. "I don't think this is going to work, kiddos. I guess there isn't enough sun coming down into this alley."

I picked up a small box. It was about as long as my thumb and about half as wide. It must have been pretty old, because the cardboard had faded from red to pink. I could barely make out the letters that said: "HIPPO'S: HOME OF THE WORLD-FAMOUS HIPPO-BURGER." There was a cartoon of a hippopotamus beneath the lettering.

"What a cute drawing," I said as I tried to open the funny little box. I shoved at one end, and a little drawer came out. "Would this help?" I asked, taking out a wooden match.

117

Chris slapped me on the back. "You worked the miracle this time."

Auntie took the little matchbox. "I used to eat there, but that closed before you kids were born."

"That tells you how long it's been since they cleaned out this room," I said. Auntie checked inside the box. "There's just this one. Any more matchboxes?"

Evie checked, but the rest of the stuff in the can was just regular junk. "We only get one try."

"Then let's make it a good one," Auntie said.

At her direction, Chris and I made a pile of stuff in the can in the middle of the cement floor, well away from the firecrackers, while Evie twisted a sheet of paper until it was like a short rope. As Evie made a second rope, Auntie broke open a package of firecrackers, which were tiny, more for noise than anything else. These she left next to the can.

Wetting her coat down with water from one of the taps over the metal sink, she handed it to me. "Get on the floor by the window, kiddos. You can get some air there. It's going to get smoky real fast."

Grandpa Eng shuffled over to the spot where Chris, Evie, and I were kneeling together. Putting our heads together, we found that we could use the coat to cover our noses and mouths. The cloth smelled like Auntie.

Carefully Auntie struck the match against the black strip on the box's side. When she didn't have any luck, she tried again.

"Now we know why it got thrown away," I said.

"I used up the sulfur on this side." Exasperated, Auntie

turned the match between her fingers and tried again. "I guess it's back to the glass," she said.

"Let me try," Grandpa Eng said. Putting a hand against the wall, he shoved himself upright. "I light kitchen fire all time back in China," he explained, shuffling over to Auntie.

Before he took the match, he limbered up his fingers some more. Once he was holding the match, he carefully turned it so that the good side was toward the matchbox that Auntie held for him.

With a quick flick of his wrist, he drew the match along the side.

I almost gave a cheer when I saw the match flare into life.

"Don't move," Auntie cautioned softly. "We don't want the flame going out."

Then, not daring to breathe, Auntie slowly held a paper rope up against Grandpa Eng's match. The dry paper caught almost immediately.

Auntie held the rope up as if she were the Statue of Liberty. "Get back against the wall," Auntie told him.

As soon as Grandpa Eng had joined us behind the coat, Auntie dropped the flaming paper rope into the can.

Little ribbons of smoke began to rise, and a moment later flames began to crackle within the can. Auntie lit the second rope from the fire and then held it against a string of firecrackers. I heard the fuse start to sizzle, and Auntie threw it against the door.

Pop! Bang!

"Fire!" Auntie shouted. We added our voices to hers.

Flames were shooting from the can now, and smoke was pouring out. Some of it went underneath the door into the sandwich shop.

Hurriedly, Auntie scurried over to us and joined us behind the coat, huddling by the window, where a cool draft of air swept through the hole.

I could hear excited shouts and a general stampede on the other side of the door. When no one opened the door, I assumed they had scurried for the street. Well, I didn't expect any of them to be heroes.

When the firecrackers had finished exploding, Auntie started to crawl forward with her coat over her mouth. When she got to the can, she picked it up with the coat and brought it over to the sink, where she poured water into it.

Even when the flames were out, the room was still filled with smoke. Picking up her trusty can of lard, Auntie went over to the door and brought the can down hard on the doorknob. I heard a clunk, but the knob stayed there.

"Try again," I said, coughing.

Auntie hit the doorknob a dozen times before she rested her arms. "All that's done is dent the can," Auntie said, panting as she examined it in disgust.

"And not a scratch on the doorknob," I said, checking it.

Auntie hit it a dozen more times before she had to rest again. "What'd they make that doorknob out of? A tank?" she said, puffing.

"Let me spell you," Chris said, taking the can from her. "Oof. This can's a lot heavier than it looks." But he managed to raise it over his head.

He was just starting to bring it down when the door opened. Chris had just enough time to see Marie's startled face. "Don't hit me!" she screamed. "I came to help you."

Chris managed to twist aside, letting go of the can so that it went flying against a shelf and knocked over a row of cans there.

Marie stepped back, shaken. "Where's the fire?"

"It was instant special effects," I said, stepping out into the sandwich shop. There seemed to be almost as much smoke here as in the storage room. No wonder the gang had gotten scared. Marie must have been just as frightened, but she had come back. Now there was a real hero.

"Thanks for saving us," I said.

Auntie came out with her bag. "Where's the gang?" she asked.

Marie made a scattering motion with her hands. "Gone."

"Do you know where my bag is?" Auntie asked.

Marie pointed to the counter, where both Auntie's and Evie's bags were. To my relief, the autograph books were there as well. I was relieved because it would still be safe to see my friends.

As we got our things, the fire engines were just arriving. We could hear Ivan banging frantically on the closet door.

There was a large crowd on the opposite side of the street as Auntie strolled out of the shop. "Don't worry about the fire, boys," Auntie told the firefighters. "But there's a lot of illegal firecrackers in there, along with a very frightened murderer."

Ignoring the onlookers, we sat down on the curb and took deep breaths of fresh air.

As soon as he had his wind back, Grandpa Eng bowed to Auntie. "Thank you, Tiger Lil. You save my grandson."

I realized something, though. "But Nick was dead before today. So who put the bullets in the gun?"

"Maybe Ivan," Grandpa Eng suggested hopefully.

"You saw how Ivan operated," Auntie said gently. "He had to stick around to pretend to make calls to Nick. He couldn't take a chance of not being around. Something might have come up, and he wouldn't have wanted one of the gang trying to reach Nick."

"So we're back to square one?" I asked, feeling sorry for Grandpa Eng.

"I'm afraid so," Auntie admitted.

"My grandson still in trouble," Grandpa Eng said. "I break another promise." Slowly he drew up his knees and rested his face against them. Suddenly his shoulders began to shake, and I heard him sobbing.

I got up to comfort Grandpa Eng, and I saw Auntie doing the same thing. However, Chris beat us to it.

"I'm so sorry," Chris said, and to my surprise he began to cry too. He leaned against the old man, repeating "sorry" over and over.

I don't think Chris realized that if Ivan hadn't put the bullets in the gun, then he was still on the hook too.

CHAPTER THIRTEEN

B y the time we finished talking to the police and the firefighters, it was the height of rush hour. The bus crawled along through the traffic, and when we got to Chinatown, it got stuck like a fly in glue.

"I might as well let you off here, folks. Nothing's moving for a while," the driver shouted.

Standing next to me, Auntie whispered, "My dogs are killing me, kiddo."

"You can soak them in a nice warm bath as soon as we get home," I promised in a low voice.

Auntie yawned. "I wish I could, but this is for Chris and Grandpa Eng," she said as we joined the flood of passengers getting off.

I knew what she meant. I was ready to sleep for the next twenty-four hours myself. And I was getting tired of lugging around all the autograph books. But what would we do about Chris and Eng?

However, as we stepped onto the sidewalk, a girl grabbed her friend excitedly. "Isn't that Clark Tom?"

Her friend stood on tiptoe to see over the crowd. "Where, where?"

I saw the reason that the bus couldn't get through. The crowd of spectators was now so large that it had spilled over into the street, tying up traffic.

Evie bit her lip as she surveyed the crowd. "How are we ever going to get through that mob?"

"Excuse us," Chris said politely, but no one moved. They didn't even bother to turn their heads.

"You leave to me," Grandpa Eng said. "Maybe you shop nice supermarket. Big, big aisles. I shop Chinatown. I do this." Lifting his elbows, he began to force his way through the crowd. He was like one of those big special boats that plow their way through the ice over the Arctic Ocean.

As I trailed Auntie through the mob, I said to her, "The show started filming this morning. How can they still be doing it?"

"Between the shooting and Leo malfunctioning, they probably fell behind their schedule," Auntie explained as we wormed our way through the crowd. "Television shows aren't like movies. Sometimes it's like being in a factory on a conveyor belt. All an actor can do is just go from one scene to another."

"The more I learn about being a star, the more I feel sorry for you and Clark," I said.

"There are times when it's not much fun," Auntie admitted, bouncing off someone's hip.

However, when we were about twenty feet from the barricades, we saw that everyone was packed so tightly that even Grandpa's elbows ran out of magic.

"I live here. Let me through," Grandpa Eng shouted, but everyone ignored him.

"Tiger Lil, where have you been?" Manny called. I saw him framed in the doorway of Clark's trailer. It was high enough to give him a good view of the crowd.

The next moment he stepped back so Clark could take his place. "Tiger Lil, come over here," he said, waving for us to come over to the trailer.

When the crowd recognized Clark, there was an excited ripple. "We love you, Clark," a woman yelled.

And there were a few cries of "Gotcha."

Clark waved his hand halfheartedly while he waited for us. "Let those people through," he called to the police.

Heads began turning as people tried to see who Clark was talking to. A woman who had been trying to knock my ribs in bubbled, "Could I have your autograph?"

At first I thought she was talking to Auntie, but then I realized she meant me, because Auntie was already past her.

"I'm nobody," I said.

However, the woman was already thrusting an autograph book and a pen at me. "Come on."

"Sure," I said. It was funny to get a little glow from Clark's spotlight.

"How about me?" a girl asked, holding up her autograph book.

From the other side of the barricade, Auntie snagged my arm. "Come on, kiddo. Later please," she said to the women. "Clark needs us."

It was even odder to hear cries of disappointment.

"Sorry," I said as Auntie dragged me off.

It might have taken a while to get to the trailer if a couple of policemen hadn't come out to escort us. As it was, someone picked my pocket. "I got her handkerchief," she said excitedly. I saw the white square waving about frantically in someone's hand.

"Fans can be strange," I said to Auntie, feeling as if I had just gone through the rollers and brushes of a car wash.

Auntie tidied my hair. "But you feel a little flattered too, don't you?"

"Well, yeah." I grinned. I thought I understood Clark a little better.

"Wasn't that neat?" Evie bubbled. She must have gotten through the souvenir hunters intact.

Chris seemed stunned, though. "That was like a football scrimmage. Is it like this all the time, Auntie?"

Amused, Auntie helped straighten Chris' collar. "Stardom isn't for sissies."

"It's scary," Chris said, still shaken by what we had gone through.

I brushed myself off, sure there were fans' fingerprints all over my clothes. "You get used to it if you hang around Auntie." That was an exaggeration, but Chris had been so negative about Auntie's career that I thought he deserved it.

Chris looked at Auntie with even more respect. "You know, you could do a lot of good if you spoke out on causes."

"We'll talk about it sometime," Auntie said. "In the meantime, Clark's waiting."

Clark himself gave Auntie a hand climbing up the steps to the trailer. "We were wondering where you went." When Grandpa Eng hesitated at the foot of the steps, Clark waved him in. "If you're a friend of Tiger Lil's, come on too."

Grandpa Eng stayed where he was. *Do you know what happened to my grandson?* he asked in Chinese. When Clark looked blank, he repeated the question in broken English.

"Who's he?" Clark asked Auntie.

"The grandfather of the kid who tried to shoot you," Auntie explained.

Grandpa Eng bowed several times. "Sorry, sorry."

"It's okay. I'm alive; and in a weird way, it was good for me. After nearly getting shot, I started to think about some things."

"My grandson?" Grandpa Eng asked.

"I think the police are charging him with the shooting," Clark said.

"Tiger Lil . . ." Grandpa Eng pleaded.

Though it had been a long day, Auntie reassured him. "We'll look for more clues in just a moment."

Clark motioned Grandpa Eng inside. "Why don't you have something to drink? Hey, Evie. Still around. Good."

"I'll . . . um . . . wait outside," Chris said nervously.

"So it's the boxing champ," Clark said, and waved him up as well. "Come on. No hard feelings?"

"No," Chris said, looking relieved.

When I stepped inside, I saw Manny busy typing away furiously at a laptop. He didn't look up from the screen.

"Can't talk. Changes for tomorrow."

Eddy waved to us from the couch. "How are you doing?"

Clark headed toward the kitchen and opened the refrigerator. "Anyone want a soda?"

"Uh . . . sure," Auntie said, startled. "How about a root beer?"

"How about you, Lily?" Clark asked.

I was speechless at having Clark Superstar waiting on me. Why was Eddy sitting?

Clark understood our expressions. "I need the exercise." Holding the refrigerator door open, he handed Auntie's drink to her and then stepped to the side so I could make my own selection. "Like I said, I've been thinking. When you have everybody going 'Yes, sir' all the time, you begin to believe you can do anything." He grinned at Eddy. "Besides, I don't want to overwork my buddy."

"We've been pals since kindergarten," Eddy said.

"Without Eddy, I wouldn't have become a star," Clark said.

Eddy squirmed. "They don't want to hear that old publicity story."

"It's the truth," Clark said. "You deserve the credit." He looked at us. "Eddy was the actor. When he went to the audition, I just tagged along."

"I told you all along that you had talent," Eddy said, "but you wouldn't try out for the school productions."

Clark shook his head and gave the grin that sent hearts fluttering all around the country. "I've got good looks. You've got the talent. You should be a star in your own right."

Eddy shook his head energetically. "And get shot at? No thank you."

"And it's high time I did right by you when we get back to L.A. I'm going to pull a few strings and get you some auditions." Clark winked at me. "So what would you like, Lily?"

For a moment, Clark could have been any teenager standing in his parents' kitchen. "A ginger ale would be nice," I said.

"Gotcha," Clark said, and got out the sodas. "What about you, sir?"

"Just water," Grandpa Eng said.

Clark waved a hand at the refrigerator's riches. "But we've got something for everyone's taste."

Grandpa Eng clicked his tongue. "Soda bad for you. Hurt your stomach. Water better."

Clark held his hands up in surrender. "Okay, okay. You win." He nodded to Eddy. "What about you, Eddy?"

"A beer," Eddy said.

"Domestic or international?" Clark asked.

"American for me," Eddy said.

When everyone was sitting on the sofas, Clark sniffed the air. "I smell smoke. Is some restaurant barbecuing?"

"I think that's us," Auntie confessed, and she told Clark what had happened to us at the sandwich shop. As she talked, Manny stopped typing to listen.

"Tiger Lil was a real tiger!" Evie said.

Clark sipped some coffee. "See, Manny? That's why you've got to get her to talk to you. She's got a whole season's worth of stories."

Manny nodded thoughtfully. "Maybe as a consultant."

Grandpa Eng set his glass down. I don't think he had touched his water. "Thank you. I find more clues now."

Guiltily, Auntie set down her soda. "I've got to go too."

Evie glanced at her watch. "Look at the time. I've got to be home for dinner."

Chris looked torn between Evie and Auntie. "I should walk you there, but Auntie might need help."

"We're just going to ask some questions, kiddo. Take Evie home," Auntie urged.

"I'll be back as soon as I can," Chris promised. "Don't do anything without me." He actually looked worried.

"Wouldn't think of it, kiddo," Auntie said, stifling a yawn.

We said our good-byes and then watched Chris and Evie leave the set. She had her arm through his and was leaning her head on his shoulder.

"She's going to be around our home all the time now," I moaned.

Auntie was smiling. "Chris looks ten feet tall right now." She pinched the bridge of her nose.

"You look exhausted, Auntie," I said. "Can't this wait until tomorrow?"

Auntie glanced at the anxious old man. "I should talk to Carl some more. I'd sure like to know who brought him his breakfast. But all I seem to be doing is walking into dead ends," she said glumly.

We went over to the prop trailer. Carl was inside, humming as he tinkered with a miniature rat on wheels.

For once, Carl was in a good mood. "Come around

tomorrow, Tiger Lil. You can see Jonathan do his tricks on camera."

"Can't wait, Carl, but do rats usually have bow ties?" Auntie asked.

Carl pulled the bow tie out by its elastic. "Naw, this is his everyday wear. He'll be in costume tomorrow."

"How did Leo work?" Auntie asked.

Carl formed a circle with his thumb and index finger. "Superb. Just one take. He made his papa proud." I noticed that his "child" had been dumped into a corner with other props he didn't need now.

"Leo's a trouper," Auntie agreed. "So do you have some spare time now, Carl?"

"What did you have in mind?" Carl asked. "I do have to get ready for tomorrow."

"I was hoping you could go to the catering tables and see if you recognize the man who brought you your breakfast," Auntie said.

"I told you. I didn't see his face," Carl said, making an adjustment with a tiny screwdriver.

"Come on, Carl," Auntie coaxed. "You can't live off air. You've got to eat sometime, and maybe you'll see something that'll jar your memory."

Carl put down a small screwdriver. "I guess it's time to get dinner anyway. Have you tried any of it yet? The food's great." Apparently he didn't share Clark's opinion about the caterer.

As we joined the line by the catering table, Carl scanned the caterers. "Nope, I don't see the old guy." He licked his lips. "Hope they've got chicken salad."

"How old?" Auntie asked.

"I don't know, but he had liver spots on his hands," Carl said.

That definitely left out Nick or Ivan.

"I wish you'd told me that before," Auntie said, annoyed.

"You didn't ask," Carl said.

I almost said that this was because he was so grouchy this morning, but I bit my tongue.

"But why would an old man frame your grandson?" I asked Grandpa Eng. "Unless," I added thoughtfully, "he's the mastermind behind some rival gang."

"You see too many kung fu movies," Grandpa Eng said.

Actually, I'd gotten the idea from Mom's favorite soap opera. "I guess we'll find out when we catch him."

"I hope soon," Grandpa Eng said.

In the meantime, Carl had picked up three of the boxes and a diet soda while Auntie cornered one of the caterers. "I'm looking for an older man who might work for your company. He might have liver spots on his hands."

The woman thought a moment. "No, I don't know anyone like that who works for the company."

A young man came by pushing a trailer with a new urn of coffee. "What about Mr. Chan? He was here this morning to check up on us."

The woman turned to Auntie. "Maybe you mean the owner, Mr. Chan?"

"Was he delivering boxes?" Auntie asked.

The two workers laughed.

"Yeah, I wish I had a camera," the woman said. "Usually

he just stands there giving orders. I've never seen him pitch in like he did this morning."

"I was surprised to see him," the young man said. "He's usually playing mah-jong day and night."

I wondered why Mr. Chan had suddenly become so helpful to his staff. So did Auntie. "Was he very upset over Clark's claim about food poisoning?" she asked.

"Sure, who wouldn't be?" the woman said. "I'd like to poison that spoiled brat myself."

I wanted to jump up and down with excitement over the new clue, but I copied Auntie, who tried to sound calm as she asked, "Do you know where I can find Mr. Chan?"

"He got disgusted when he heard we were being fired. He said he was going to forget his sorrows in a good game of mah-jong. He ought to be there right now," the woman said, and she wrote down his address and gave it to Auntie.

I looked around for Carl, but he must have already left to work on his next prop. Auntie snagged two dinner boxes. The food smelled so good that I got one myself.

"Here. You might as well eat," Auntie said, holding out one of the boxes to Grandpa Eng.

He shook his head. *"I can't take the film company's food. They accused my grandson of murder."*

"But you heard Clark. He doesn't hold a grudge against you," I said.

Grandpa Eng shook his head. *"You're either upright or you're not."* He used a Chinese word that meant "virtuous" but also "straight as a ruler." *"I haven't been, but I'm going to change. Starting from now."*

I held out my hand. "I'll take the other box back."

Auntie turned so that her body was between me and the boxes. "I got to get into shape for my role, kiddo. I'm keeping this." She opened the lid of one of them. "Hmm, yummy. Fried chicken."

As we walked through the set, we ate our dinners—some of us more than others. When I didn't eat my tapioca pudding, Auntie even had mine. "But you hate tapioca," I said.

"This body craves sugar, kiddo," Auntie said, tossing it down.

She was shameless. Whenever she found someone with an uneaten tapioca, she asked for it.

"I should have decided to do character roles years ago," she said, smacking her lips.

"So why would Mr. Chan personally deliver a breakfast to Carl?" I wondered. "If I was going to baby anyone, it'd be Clark. After all, Clark is the one who says they gave him food poisoning."

Auntie paused in midsmack. "But what if he was mad at Clark? After all, Clark wanted to break the catering contract."

I thought about that. "He'd be out a lot of money."

"He'd lose even more if word got out—and it would." Auntie ate another spoonful. "Other clients would hear and maybe drop him. He could be ruined."

"That make me real mad," Grandpa Eng said, coming to the same conclusion. "I very mad at Clark then."

"Maybe Mr. Chan was mad enough to rig the gun with real bullets when Carl wasn't looking," I said.

"I think it's time we play a little mah-jong," Auntie said, flexing her fingers.

"*Mah-jong has always been my game.*" Grandpa Eng grinned.

"Then let's go find Carl's friend," Auntie said grimly.

"We promised to wait for Chris," I reminded her.

"We don't have the time," Auntie said, shaking her head.

"Do you think it's getting worse for Chris and Eng?" I asked.

"If we don't solve this case soon," Auntie said grimly, "we'd better learn how to bake cakes with files in them."

CHAPTER FOURTEEN

The address turned out to be some sort of social club housed in a three-story building on the south side of a row of buildings squeezed together between Sacramento Street on the south and Clay Street on the north. The club itself fronted a narrow little alley on the east. At its rear was another row of buildings that faced west to Stockton.

The clacking of mah-jong tiles slipped through the open windows and echoed against the walls.

When I saw the plume of smoke drifting through the windows, I asked Auntie, "Is it on fire?"

Auntie sniffed the air. "No. It's cigarette smoke. Some of the older Chinese haven't gotten the word on smoking yet."

It took a couple of buzzes at the doorbell before we heard footsteps coming down some stairs. "Yes?" a voice asked. The door muffled the sound a bit.

"We're looking for a Mr. Chan. He owns a catering company," Auntie said through the wood.

"He's busy," the man said.

"Ah Sam," Grandpa Eng said. "Is that you?"

The door opened a crack, and an eyeball stared at Grandpa Eng. "I haven't seen you in a long time."

"I keep busy," Grandpa Eng said. "Can we come up?"

Ah Sam opened the door. He was a short, bald man in his fifties, and he was dressed in an old gray sweater and slacks. On his feet were a pair of plastic sandals.

"You can, but I don't know these two," Ah Sam said.

Grandpa Eng waved a hand at Auntie. "Don't you know who this is? It's the famous Tiger Lil."

A broad smile spread across Ah Sam's face. "Ah, Feet of Fury," he said, pointing at Auntie. "Why didn't you just kick the door down?"

Auntie grinned. "My bursitis is acting up. This is my great-niece," she said, turning to me.

Ah Sam nodded in a friendly way to me. "Come up. How's your mah-jong?"

Auntie started to climb the stairs. "I think I can still pung with the best of them, but my chi-ing is a little rusty." I didn't play mah-jong, but I'd watched my mom play with her friends, so I knew those were terms from the game.

"We'll rub the rust off you fast," Ah Sam said, and he rubbed his hands together. "Did you bring any money?"

"We just came to see Mr. Chan," Auntie said.

Ah Sam looked curious as we went up the steps. "He never told me he knew anyone that famous."

He led us into a narrow, smoky room filled with people about his age. A quarter of them were smoking, and several had the biggest cigars I'd ever seen. They were seated around a half dozen tables on which I saw the walls built by two layers of mah-jong tiles. The players all looked very serious.

Long fluorescent lights ran along the ceiling, and there was an old refrigerator gurgling away in one corner. On a table next to it was a big urn and a box of tea bags. A woman was filling a cup with hot water from the urn.

"*Everyone, everyone,*" Ah Sam called. When he had gotten their attention, he pointed at Auntie. "*Mr. Chan, Tiger Lil is here to see you.*"

A woman got up from her seat. "*Oh, I Remember Amah.*"

"*Yes, I was in that film,*" Auntie said modestly.

Mr. Chan was a man in his sixties. He'd hung his catering jacket over the back of his chair, and he had liver spots on the backs of his hands. "*What do you want with me?*" he asked, looking puzzled.

"*We just want to ask you a few questions,*" Auntie said. "*Did you see anything suspicious when you were in the prop room on the set of* East Meets West?"

He shook his head fiercely. "*I was never there.*"

"*You know, where they're shooting Clark Tom's show,*" Auntie said.

He bent over the row of tiles in front of him. "*I'm the boss. I hire other people to do the dirty work.*"

That wasn't what his own employees had said.

"*But—*" Grandpa Eng began.

Auntie held up a hand, gesturing for him to be quiet. "*Let me handle this,*" she whispered to him. Then she said to Mr. Chan, "*Thank you. I guess we were mistaken.*"

Giving us the eye, Auntie turned and started for the door.

"*Wait*," Ah Sam said. "*Mr. Chan, don't you want her autograph for your granddaughter?*"

"*No,*" Mr. Chan said, without looking up.

"*But you told me how she's crazy about film stars,*" Ah Sam said to him, and then he turned to Auntie. "*She wants to go to Hollywood.*"

"*Who doesn't?*" Auntie said, studying Mr. Chan suspiciously. "*Well, if you'll excuse us . . .*"

"*Do you have to go already?*" Ah Sam asked. "*We were looking for some people to start another game.*" He indicated a table next to Mr. Chan's that was piled with green-backed tiles.

Suddenly Auntie looked thoughtful. "*I've got time. Do you?*" she asked Grandpa Eng.

He followed her lead. "*Sure.*"

"*Wonderful!*" Ah Sam pulled a chair out for Auntie.

Auntie whispered to me in a low, gravelly voice like some police officer. "*We'll stake him out.*"

"*Roger. Ten-four,*" I whispered back. That was police talk I'd heard on one of the police shows.

Ah Sam waited by the chair, ready to slide it underneath her, but Auntie ignored him and selected a chair that would let her stare directly at Mr. Chan, at his own table.

Ah Sam stood there uncertainly and then sat down himself in the chair he had drawn out. "*We need a fourth to finish out the game,*" he said to me.

"*I not know how,*" I confessed in my broken Chinese.

Grandpa Eng shook his head in disgust. *"Shameful."* It seemed to be his favorite word whenever he spoke about younger people.

"I always too busy," I said. To be honest, it was what little old Chinatown people played. Give me a video game anytime.

"Don't worry. We'll teach you." Auntie patted the seat of the remaining chair.

"We usually play for a penny a point," Ah Sam said, scratching his nose.

That seemed harmless enough, but Auntie said, *"Would it be all right if we didn't? My great-niece is a beginner."*

"But money makes it more fun," Ah Sam complained. I guessed there were tile sharks as well as card sharks.

Grandpa Eng folded his arms. *"You haven't learned a thing in forty years, have you? You never play for money with two strangers. How do you know we won't feed winning hands to one another?"*

"But I trust you," Ah Sam protested.

"Don't," Grandpa Eng advised mischievously, and he nodded at me. *"You especially never play with strangers who say they don't know the game."*

Ah Sam squinted at me good-naturedly. *"She does look a little suspicious."*

Auntie picked up one of the mah-jong tiles. The face was of some material yellowed with age. On it was a peacock with the number one in Chinese.

"It's made out of bone," she said. *"I like those better than plastic."* She set it back, facedown.

"They make a more satisfying sound," Ah Sam agreed.

Spreading his hands over the table, he began to swirl the tiles around so that they made a clacking sound.

"Come on," Auntie said. "This is how we mix up the tiles. It's the same thing as shuffling a deck of cards."

When I saw Auntie and Grandpa Eng do the same thing, I also stretched out my hands. It was funny, but there was something soothing about the tiles. They felt so cool and pleasant to the touch; and the solid little tiles bumped together in a pleasing way. And there was something relaxing in just moving your arms around in slow circles.

Then, by some silent communication, the three adults stopped mixing the tiles and began stacking them in rows, two high, so I did the same. When that was finished, we shook dice to see who would become the "East Wind." "That's the one who gets to play first," Auntie said; and as it happened, she was it.

Then she "broke" the wall by beginning to select her tiles. We took turns until each of us had fourteen tiles in front of each of us.

"The basic game's like gin rummy," Auntie explained. "A chi is three tiles of the same suit in sequence. A pung is three of a kind. The goal is to get four chis or pungs in combination and two of a kind. You can only pick up the discard of the person who played ahead of you—unless it's the tile that you need to win. Then you can grab the discard of anyone."

There were a lot more rules that I forgot as soon as Auntie told me. "What's this?" I asked, holding up one of my tiles.

"A green dragon," Auntie said. "There's only four of them in the game."

"And this?" I asked.

"A red dragon."

Auntie set down a couple of very pretty tiles. *"These are flower tiles. They add points,"* she said. Then she took two from the wall to take their place. *"Anyone else?"* But no one else took any.

Auntie made her discard, and we began. We play a lot of gin rummy and hearts in the family, so some parts of the game seemed familiar. The game went pretty fast, and in no time Grandpa Eng was laying his tiles facedown. *"I eat!"* he said.

"That means he won," Auntie explained to me.

"You bet I did," Grandpa Eng said, beaming triumphantly.

Ah Sam leaned over and whistled admiringly as he studied Grandpa's winning hand. *"Three thousand one hundred."*

That was thirty-one dollars. Suddenly I was glad that we weren't playing for money. After a few games, when Auntie and Grandpa Eng racked up the points, I think Ah Sam was grateful too.

All this time, from the corner of my eye, I'd been keeping an eye on Mr. Chan. He'd been getting more and more nervous the longer we stayed.

At a break between games he got up slowly. As one Auntie, Grandpa Eng, and I rose too. Mr. Chan immediately flopped back into his seat.

Ah Sam cleared his throat politely. *"Shall we play?"*

I saw then that Auntie and Grandpa Eng were also both staring at Mr. Chan with radar eyes. No wonder he'd been startled.

If we hadn't been in the middle of a stakeout and all

the smoke, I could have really enjoyed myself. The people had come to gossip and have a good time more than to play. There was a lot of good-natured teasing when anyone lost or won. And there were a lot of Chinatown memories to share among people who had lived here all their lives.

I began to hear a kind of music when we mixed the tiles together—like it was a xylophone made out of little bones. And the laughter and the gossip and the stories were part of that music.

Eventually, I got a good hand. I started out with a lot of pairs to begin with; and when Ah Sam made a discard, I picked it up. "*I think I win,*" I said, and I laid them out. "*I mean, I eat.*"

Ah Sam slapped his head. "*Sixty thousand points,*" he said.

"*Maybe we should play for money.*" I grinned.

Grandpa Eng elbowed his friend. "*See? I told you not to trust her.*"

"*I won't,*" Ah Sam said, eyeing me suspiciously.

"*This game not bad once you learn,*" I said. I liked figuring out the odds. I even liked the feel of the tiles. It was fun in a different way than a video game.

"*Chinatown's the same way,*" Grandpa Eng said. "*Traditions, stories—you should learn them all.*"

In my heart I knew Grandpa Eng was right, of course; but I didn't want to give him the satisfaction of telling him that, so I just shrugged. "*Maybe I will.*"

"*Young people,*" Grandpa Eng said, making a disgusted sound in his throat.

"*I know. Shameful, shameful,*" I said.

Mr. Chan, in the meantime, had gotten even more upset as our stakeout went on. His trembling fingers kept knocking over his tiles, exposing his hand, to the delight of the other players.

"*Where is your mind tonight?*" a woman teased. "*You haven't won one game.*"

Our stakeout must have finally gotten to our suspect. Suddenly he sprang to his feet. From beneath his chair he picked up a pink plastic bag.

Immediately we three got up too.

"*My right leg's gone to sleep,*" Grandpa Eng said, and he started to wriggle it. "*My circulation's not as good as it used to be.*"

"*You're getting old,*" Ah Sam teased.

"*Then treat me with respect, you young punk.*" Grandpa Eng pointed at his gray hairs. "*They mean I'm wise.*"

Ah Sam was unimpressed. "*They just mean you're too cheap to buy hair dye.*"

Grandpa Eng jerked his head at Ah Sam's glistening dome. "*You're just jealous because I have hair.*"

While the two had been joking, Mr. Chan had gone over to the urn of hot water. He'd made a point of not looking at us as he made himself a cup of tea.

Gritting his teeth, he deliberately spilled some tea on himself. "*Ah-h, ah-h,*" he groaned.

"*Did you burn yourself?*" a nearby woman asked.

"*No, but I got to clean up,*" Mr. Chan said. "*I spilled tea on my pants leg.*" He hurried down a hall.

The circulation immediately came back to Grandpa's leg, and he set his foot down on the floor. "*Where's the

144

men's room?" he asked Ah Sam.

"Third door to your right," Ah Sam said, nodding. Somehow, despite his bad leg, Grandpa Eng managed to break into a run.

"My goodness. He must have to go very badly," Ah Sam said as he watched Grandpa Eng.

Auntie started to follow. "I should powder my nose."

"Me too," I said, leaping after her.

Ah Sam seemed surprised that we would all have to use the rest room at the same time. "We only have one toilet," he said.

"Any windows to it?" Auntie asked.

Ah Sam was just plain puzzled by that. "No. Does that matter?"

"No," Auntie said, but I knew it meant there was only one way out for Mr. Chan.

As we hurried after Grandpa Eng, I couldn't help giggling. "He's going to think we have to go real bad too."

Auntie muttered to me, "Let him think what he likes, kiddo. I just want to find out why Mr. Chan lied through his teeth."

I glanced over my shoulder. Ah Sam was peeking at our hands. "Ah Sam also cheats."

"All's fair in love and mah-jong," Auntie said.

Unfortunately that was also true about a certain angry caterer.

We had just got to the doorway when we heard someone say, "Ow!" followed by an ominous thump.

CHAPTER FIFTEEN

Grandpa Eng was lying in the hallway. "*Are you all right?*" Auntie asked, rushing over to him.

He sat up slowly, swearing. He had a shiner to match Clark's. "*He was waiting for me when I got to the hallway. He hit me with his bag. Whatever he's got in that thing, it's heavy.*"

Auntie and I helped him get to his feet; then Grandpa Eng shook us off. "*Hurry. We've got to catch him.*"

Ah Sam came out that moment. "*Someone said they heard a noise.*" He stared at Grandpa Eng when he saw the black eye. "*What happened to you?*"

"*I fell,*" Grandpa Eng fibbed.

"*Yes, well. It's really been nice, but we lost track of the time. We have to go. Thanks so much for the hospitality,*" Auntie blurted out.

"*You all finished so soon?*" Ah Sam asked, even more bewildered.

"*No time for pleasantries either,*" Auntie said, heading for the stairs. "*We wanted to apologize to Mr. Chan for the mistake.*"

146

"He has to be in here somewhere," Ah Sam said, taking out a set of keys. "I got the only key to the front door. I have to let everyone in or out. We had to start doing that after the Powell Street Boys forced their way into another place and robbed everyone."

Grandpa Eng looked a little guilty over what his grandson's gang had done.

"You not help what grandson did," I whispered.

"I should have raised him properly," he mumbled, and he shook his head miserably.

I thought Auntie was going to stay in the hallway, but she kept on walking. "Well, then please give our apologies to him. I'm afraid we can't wait for him."

As Ah Sam let us out, he called, "Please come back anytime." He winked at me. "But with you, I won't play for money, so don't even try to suggest it."

As soon as we were outside, I gratefully took in deep lungfuls of air. "There was so much smoke, it was like being in a chimney. They should close that place as an environmental hazard."

Overhead the clouds in the twilit sky were a purplish gray. I hoped we had enough light to see.

"Why didn't you wait for Mr. Chan?" Grandpa Eng asked Auntie in frustration.

"Because he might have already left the building. The lock on the door to the roof might not need a key from the inside." Auntie craned her neck back to look up at the rooftops. "Or if he's still hiding inside, my guess is that he won't stay too long."

"He'll expect us to be waiting by the front door," I said.

"Should one of us stake out the back door?"

Auntie pantomimed squeezing something between her two hands. "This block is a typical Chinatown block. There's two rows of buildings jammed together, so they don't have rear exits." She pointed to another door twenty feet away from the first. "That's what serves as a back door. It probably leads to the garbage cans with a staircase that will take you up to the rear of the building."

I studied the buildings too. "The only other way he could get out would be the fire escape." Every building had a fire escape built across its front. I guessed that was because the buildings were built so close together.

Auntie rubbed her chin. "But once he got to the rooftop of the social club, he could cross the rooftops to the row of buildings to the west. Then he could climb down the fire escape of one of those to Stockton."

"So we split up and each take a street?" I asked.

Auntie pointed at either end of the alley. "Two of us could stand at the opposite ends of the alley. That way one can keep an eye on Sacramento Street and the alley while the other can watch Clay Street and the alley. The third person can watch on Stockton. That way we can cover all the escape routes."

"I take that side of the alley." Grandpa Eng pointed to the Clay Street mouth.

"I'll take Stockton," I said. That was on the opposite side of the building.

"That's too dangerous." Auntie shook her head. "I wish I'd asked Chris to come."

"I can run even faster than he can," I said.

148

"Well," Auntie said reluctantly, "if you see Mr. Chan, come and get me. Don't do anything stupid."

As I headed up the alley and on to Sacramento Street, I thought to myself if anyone should listen to her own warning, it was Auntie.

I leaned against a streetlamp on one corner where I could keep an eye on Auntie, who was waiting at the mouth of the alley by Sacramento Street. I assumed Grandpa Eng had taken up his position at the alley mouth by Clay.

Overhead, the night sky was a narrow strip between the buildings. In the glare of the streetlights, you could see only a couple of stars, though. Mostly the sky was black like the street.

For a moment I imagined there was a Chinatown above us with more people. And maybe above that was another Chinatown—like the layers of an onion. Just like there were layers to people, like Grandpa Eng or Clark.

Life in Chinatown had not only gotten interesting with Auntie around; she made me see things that I never had noticed before.

I was just starting to get an ache in my neck when a blob suddenly detached itself from the shadows. As it came awkwardly down the ladder of the fire escape, I saw the catering jacket. It was Mr. Chan. Clutched in one hand was his plastic bag.

Quickly I signaled to Auntie, and then stepped out of sight around the corner. However, I kept poking my head out to check on Mr. Chan's progress. He had not been a mountain goat in a former life. He took his time coming down the fire escape. By the time he had reached the last landing, Auntie had come up Sacramento Street to stand behind me.

"Where's Grandpa Eng?" I asked.

"I waved him up the other street to box in Mr. Chan," Auntie said.

The last ladder descended with a metal clang to the sidewalk. I peeked around the corner again. "He's just starting down on the last part," I said.

"Let's go," Auntie said, moving past me.

You can't live in Chinatown and not develop muscles from climbing the hills and staircases. Auntie had gotten soft while she had been living in southern California, so that gave me a slight edge.

"Hey, Mr. Chan," I said as I ran toward him.

He froze on the last rung. Then he looked at the roof as if he didn't know whether to climb back up again or run. When he saw Auntie so far behind me, he decided to risk running. Jumping down to the sidewalk, he tried to dart along Stockton.

"Hey, stop," I said. I was taking this personally now. I ran after him.

"Come back here, kiddo," Auntie called.

Mr. Chan ran a lot faster than I would have expected him to after playing mah-jong in that smoky room all those years. He ran down the street, actually keeping the distance between us. As he galloped along, he waved an arm over his head desperately while his eyes searched the street. "Taxi, taxi."

"Don't go so fast, kiddo!" Auntie was shouting.

Suddenly a taxi shot down Clay Street across the intersection and screeched against the curb.

"He's a criminal," I shouted to the cabbie.

My words only seemed to make Mr. Chan run faster, and all the cab driver did was open his door. In a few moments he would be gone.

Anger boiled up inside me. "Stop!" I shouted.

Just as he passed the corner of the building, Mr. Chan suddenly flipped backward. Grandpa Eng stepped out, rubbing his knuckles. *"Hit me, will you?"*

The cabbie slammed the door and roared away. I guessed he'd given up on Mr. Chan as a fare.

Almost casually Grandpa Eng straddled Mr. Chan and plopped down on his stomach, pinning Mr. Chan's arms to his sides.

"Oof," Mr. Chan grunted. His eyelids blinked open, and he started to shake his head groggily.

Grandpa Eng grabbed him by the collar and raised him up halfway. *"Why did you frame my grandson?"*

Mr. Chan looked up at him, frightened. *"What grandson?"*

"Don't you try to lie anymore." Grandpa Eng held up a fist menacingly. *"Tell me."*

"I don't know what you're talking about," Mr. Chan wailed.

"Talk," Grandpa Eng ordered.

Curious, I picked up the plastic bag that had fallen from his hand.

"That's mine," Mr. Chan protested.

There were a used paper napkin, some pens, a half-eaten apple, and a heavy mug. I showed the last item to Grandpa Eng. "This must have been what knocked you down."

"*I'm sorry; I'm sorry,*" Mr. Chan began to babble.

"What's he want with this junk?" I wondered.

"One person's trash is another person's treasure, kiddo." Auntie took the mug from me and turned it so I could see the name printed on it.

"That's Clark's missing mug," I said, "but the napkin?"

"Clark wiped his mouth with it, didn't he?" Auntie asked Mr. Chan.

"Yes." Mr. Chan began to bob up and down.

"And he used the pens?" Auntie asked.

"Yes, yes." Mr. Chan nodded eagerly. "I don't care about that spoiled brat, but he's all my granddaughter talks about. So I was looking for souvenirs for her."

"Did you deliver the catering boxes yourself so you could hunt for souvenirs?" Auntie asked.

"It was my granddaughter's idea," he admitted.

Grandpa Eng let go of Mr. Chan. "*Why did you deny being on the set?*"

"Because I thought you were from the film company and wanted the stuff back," Mr. Chan said, and then he looked at us anxiously. "You're not, are you?"

Auntie looked embarrassed. I guessed we had harassed the poor man into taking a risky climb. "No. Don't worry. We won't turn you in." She held up the mug. "I've got to give this back to Clark, but I'm sure he'll give you an autographed photo."

"But my granddaughter wanted something personal," Mr. Chan said. He tried to sit up, though Grandpa Eng was still on his stomach. "And I lost the T-shirt."

"To whom?" Auntie asked intently.

Mr. Chan shook his head, almost in tears. "I don't know. This man caught me, and he threatened to call the police. That's why I was so scared when you came in."

"There were costumes in the prop room," Auntie said.

"The hamper was in there," Mr. Chan said.

"So he was in the prop room?" Auntie asked.

"Yes. He said he was from the laundry," Mr. Chan said.

"Was there anyone else in the room with you?" Auntie asked.

"A man working on a lion, but he didn't notice us," Mr. Chan said. "The laundry man spoke in a whisper. I guess he didn't want to bother the other man."

"Carl probably wouldn't notice a laundry man any more than a caterer," Auntie said.

"Not while he was working on Leo," I agreed.

"What's this all about anyway?" Mr. Chan demanded. Now that he knew we weren't official, he was starting to get angry.

So we told him the story, leaving out the fact that Grandpa's grandson was in the Powell Street Boys.

As Grandpa Eng helped him to his feet, he apologized. *"So I'm sorry about the misunderstanding."*

Mr. Chan chuckled as he pointed at Grandpa Eng's eye. *"I think you paid for it."* Then he rubbed the back of his head. *"And from the bump on my head, you gave as good as you got. I guess it is kind of my fault too."*

"I'll see that you get something nice from Clark," Auntie said.

"Something personal?" Mr. Chan asked hopefully.

"Clark's a pretty nice guy, so I'll see what I can do," Auntie said. "But do you mind telling me what the laundry man looked like?"

"Tall, thin, with gray hair." Mr. Chan pointed at a spot on his own left nostril. "Oh, and he spoke Cantonese with a northern accent."

Grandpa Eng slumped against a wall in surprise. "That my boss, Mr. Li."

CHAPTER SIXTEEN

Auntie dusted Mr. Chan off with promises to get a souvenir for his granddaughter. However, the caterer seemed more worried about Grandpa Eng. "Are you going to be all right?"

Grandpa Eng was leaning against a wall, still in shock. He nodded dumbly.

I was sorry I'd suspected Mr. Chan—and I felt even worse that I had helped hound the man into climbing down a fire escape. If they arrested every grandparent who wanted to spoil a granddaughter, the jails would be full.

"No hard feelings, right?" Mr. Chan asked Grandpa Eng. Grandpa Eng shook his head this time. Reassured, Mr. Chan handed a card to Auntie. "This has my address and phone number. Thank you."

"You'll hear from me," Auntie said, putting it away carefully.

As he walked away, Grandpa Eng scratched his head and asked, *"But why would Mr. Li try to kill Clark? He was happy with the fee the company was paying him. And they were letting him clean the costumes."*

Auntie bit her lip. *"The laundry's next to the 'court-house.' Do you suppose he overheard Clark talking to Evie about becoming a star? Maybe he couldn't stand the thought of his brother succeeding through his daughter. He only pretended not to know her."*

"Another Chinatown feud," I said.

On our last case several months ago, we'd met a woman who'd been holding a grudge for years and tried to take her revenge out on the grandsons of her enemy. Chinatown feuds ran deep.

"He hates his brother," Grandpa Eng said, sighing.

"Maybe there's a perfectly innocent explanation for your boss, just as there was for Mr. Chan," Auntie said.

He thought about that a moment. *"I don't know whether to hope that's true or not. Because if it is, we still have to find the one who framed my grandson."*

It was nighttime when we got back to the set. The company was still shooting the scenes, but a lot of the lights were gone or not lit. Most of the crowd had dispersed.

"They must be shooting the interiors now," Auntie said. All the windows of the laundry were glowing brightly.

Chris was standing near the line of cops, fuming. I guessed they wouldn't let him in.

"Why did you go off the set?" Chris called to us, upset. "I told you to wait."

"Hold it a sec," Auntie told him. She spoke to one of the cops, who must have checked with Manny and then let us through.

156

As we walked toward the laundry, Auntie said, "We had to run down a lead."

That didn't calm Chris down at all. "You think Lily can handle it but I can't?"

It's funny how quickly worry can turn to anger. "You've got your nerve giving us the third degree," I snapped. "We're doing this mostly for you."

"And I thought something had happened to you," Chris snapped back. He was starting to sound almost human. Auntie had that effect upon people if they hung around her long enough.

Inside the laundry Manny was discussing something with one of the crew. "Hey, Tiger Lil," he greeted her. "You're just in time. We're running through a scene from the beginning of the show. Clark's interrogating the owner of the laundry."

"Mr. Li?" I asked.

"No, an actor," Manny said. He led us behind the counter to a large room where a plump actor worked at a press. Clark started to walk toward him, but then the cameraman said something to Wayne. "Cut," Wayne shouted, and he got out of his chair to look through the camera.

Clark waved to us as he stood waiting for Wayne and the cameraman to finish discussing the shot. When the cameras weren't rolling, he looked exhausted.

There were about thirty crewmembers all around, with lights and silver winglike things that Auntie said were screens used to reflect the light in a certain way. The laundry itself was a jumble, with tables pushed back to make room for the camera and the recording equipment.

I'd assumed television and films were like windows into actors' lives. Now I realized what a team effort making them took. In fact, it was almost like a crew working in a factory to produce a car. Carl nodded to us with a wooden leg cradled in his arms.

In the meantime, Grandpa Eng had been getting impatient. I knew he wanted to find his boss, but when he tried to go toward the back of the laundry, Manny caught him.

"Whoa, partner. Where do you think you're going?"

"I live here," Grandpa Eng protested.

"Not tonight," Manny said. "We do."

"But my boss—" Grandpa Eng started to say.

"I just saw him," Manny said, keeping a firm grip on Grandpa Eng. I thought about warning Manny about Grandpa's haymaker, but Auntie put a hand on Grandpa's shoulder.

I guess Chris was starting to feel just as impatient. "But—" he started to protest.

"Listen to your auntie," Auntie scolded. "We have to wait for a break between scenes."

"Action," Wayne shouted.

An alarm sounded, someone shouted the next numbers for the scene, and the cameras began to roll.

Considering all the time it must have taken to set up the scene, they zipped through the shooting this try. Then a number of people had to declare themselves happy with the take, from the cameraman to the soundman and couple of other people at several machines.

"We don't have the luxury of a lot of takes, like you did on your films," Manny said to Auntie. He got a clipboard from an assistant and consulted it. "We're going to be setting up for another scene, so you probably have half an hour to find Mr. Li."

"Thanks," Auntie said.

Grandpa Eng had been practically hopping up and down with impatience. *"We'll go to the office,"* he said, and he headed off to our right.

The office was a small cubbyhole in the back next to a leaking toilet. Auntie felt a cup of tea on the desk. "It's warm."

"That's the boss' mug," Grandpa Eng said. *"He must be around."* He turned around to look for him. *"Let's try down in the basement."*

Beyond the toilet was a door leading to the "courthouse," and beyond that was a set of rickety steps.

Chris stared at them doubtfully. "How old is this staircase?"

"Since after earthquake," Grandpa Eng said.

"Which one?" Auntie asked.

"Nineteen-oh-six," Grandpa Eng said simply, as if there couldn't be any other.

As Grandpa Eng started down, Chris said, "Let me go next."

I was glad to let them test the staircase first, as I heard the treads creak dangerously beneath their feet.

The basement looked even older than the laundry

upstairs, and it smelled damp and moldy—maybe from all the steam. Big machines squatted on the concrete floor like huge monsters.

At the bottom of the stairs we paused, trying to orient ourselves, and then we heard the clink of metal.

"*It came from over here,*" Grandpa Eng said, and he moved ahead confidently through the maze of machinery. I hurried after him, wishing I had brought bread crumbs to drop behind me.

Auntie grabbed hold of my sleeve. "We don't want to get separated down here."

As the clinking got louder, Grandpa Eng started to run. "Wait," Auntie said. We didn't have any choice but to run as well, hopping over a mop that leaned against one of the machines.

Ahead of us Grandpa Eng burst into an aisle in front of a huge boiler with lots of dials. His boss, in a blue business suit, was banging away at a big valve with a wrench—I guessed to loosen it.

I was going to follow, but Auntie pulled me back. "Hold it, kiddo. We're the reserves."

"*Boss, what are you doing?*" Grandpa Eng asked.

The boss jumped up but didn't turn around. "*Go away,*" he said gruffly. He spoke Cantonese with a slight accent. I guessed that's what Mr. Chan had meant when he said Mr. Li talked with a northern accent.

Grandpa Eng leaned his head suspiciously to the side. "*You got a cold, boss?*"

"*Unh, yes.*" The boss gave a cough.

"*I need to ask you something,*" Grandpa Eng said.

"*Later*," the boss said.

"*What's wrong with the boiler?*" Grandpa Eng asked.

"*Trying to fix this pipe.*" The boss gestured to it with the wrench. "*The Hollywood people say they wants lots of steam for the shot.*"

"*But you could just do that with these valves.*" Grandpa Eng pointed to some smaller pipes with dials. "*That pipe carries the hot steam. You do that wrong, and this whole place could blow up.*"

"*Just leave me alone.*" The boss urgently began to work on the nut again.

"*Somebody could get hurt,*" Grandpa Eng said, grabbing his boss and spinning him around.

Eddy raised the wrench. "That's the idea, old man."

CHAPTER SEVENTEEN

I'd caught only a glimpse of Mr. Li earlier today, but from what I remembered of him, Eddy in a wig and blue suit resembled him. On a set he'd have had access to all the stuff he needed for a disguise, and as an actor he'd have had the skills to use it.

During the rehearsal, he'd have had enough time to put on his Mr. Li disguise and go into the prop trailer. But Mr. Chan had already been there, hunting for souvenirs. Eddy had known Carl would be absorbed with Leo, so he had scared off the only person who might have noticed him putting the real bullets into the gun.

Though he was startled, Grandpa Eng wasn't backing down. "Where Mr. Li?" he demanded.

"He's locked up in a closet. You can chat with him in just a second," Eddy said, motioning with the wrench.

However, Grandpa Eng slipped out of his reach. "You sound like Mr. Li."

"My family comes from Taiwan"—Eddy shrugged—"so it's easy to sound like him."

"So you scare him. Make him tell you how blow up laundry," Grandpa Eng said.

"You're clever, old man. Too clever," Eddy growled.

"I think it's time for the reserves to go in," Auntie whispered, snatching up the mop. "Chris, you watch your sister."

"But—" Chris began indignantly.

"No buts," Auntie said. She was already moving forward.

Chris would have followed, but I set down the autograph books and tackled him. "One lucky punch doesn't make you Superman," I hissed. "Auntie knows what she's doing." I hoped.

"But Eng really is innocent," he said, trying to pull free. "I would have just looked the other way while he got convicted, but Auntie fought for the truth. I've got to help her now."

I tightened my grip. "Quiet, or you'll call attention to us."

Reluctantly my brother stopped struggling.

By the boiler a deadly dance had begun. When he saw Auntie from the corner of his eye, Grandpa Eng shifted to the side so that Eddy's back would be to her.

"Why you frame my grandson?" Grandpa Eng asked.

Eddy crouched, getting ready to swing when he had a clear shot. "I didn't know he was your grandson."

"He one of bosses of Powell Street Boys," Grandpa Eng warned. "They be very mad when they hear what you did."

That made Eddy hesitate, but only for a moment. "Then I'd better make sure you don't leave this basement."

The deadly shuffling went on as Auntie tiptoed across the floor. "You not let Mr. Li and me leave," Grandpa Eng said. "You not want witnesses. But why?"

Eddy jerked a thumb toward his own chest. "This should have been my show," he said bitterly. "If I hadn't talked that ham into coming with me, it would have. I've put up with that spoiled brat long enough."

"But Clark nice to you now," Grandpa Eng said.

"That's today. Tomorrow's another matter," Eddy said.

Auntie was just behind Eddy. Now she raised the mop over her shoulder like she was ready to hit a home run.

Unfortunately, she swung just when Eddy did—with just about as much impact. Grandpa Eng ducked to the side so that the wrench whistled over his head. And Eddy had put so much force into his blow that he leaned forward. Auntie's mop whipped by where his head had been.

"What?" Eddy asked, and he caught the mop on the backswing. Spluttering, he backed up as Grandpa Eng hit him behind the knees. With a shout, he fell over in a tangle with Grandpa Eng. And somehow their kicking legs caught Auntie so that she fell on top of them.

"Get help," she said to us, panting. She helped Grandpa Eng wrestle Eddy, but Eddy was slippery as an eel; they couldn't pin him down despite their best efforts.

I had just turned to run when Eddy shouted, "Come out if you want her to live."

I whirled around. Eddy was still lying sandwiched between Auntie and Grandpa Eng, but he now had a gun pointed at Auntie.

Auntie jerked her head toward Chris and me. "Grandpa and I are dead anyway, kiddos. Run."

"I mean it," Eddy said savagely.

In moments like these I always try to ask myself what Auntie would do. And then I knew: She'd never save her own skin.

Chris must have figured out the same thing, because he was already stepping out into the open. I followed a moment later.

"While you're alive," Chris said confidently to Auntie, "you'll get us out of this."

Auntie groaned. "I think I've run out of miracles."

Eddy carefully untangled himself and stood up. "Why did you have to complicate things so much?" he asked, agitatedly rubbing his forehead.

"You can't put a bullet in us," Auntie said as she got up. "The police will know the boiler explosion wasn't an accident."

"Think. Think," Eddy said to himself, tapping his knuckles against his head.

Next to me, Auntie was trying just as hard to figure out a way to stop him. I tried too, but I didn't see much that we could do. Still, Auntie had gotten us out of some pretty tight spots before.

I thought about making a rush. The way Chris' shoulders were tensing, I saw that he must have been considering the same thing.

"Stay where you are," Eddy warned as he swung his gun back and forth between us. He obviously didn't think Grandpa Eng was a real threat.

"*Remember,*" Grandpa Eng murmured to Auntie. "*Save my grandson.*"

"*What are you—?*" Auntie began to ask.

However, Grandpa Eng was already lunging forward, arms outstretched, with a loud cry.

Eddy looked almost as scared as Grandpa Eng, and I think his finger tightened on the trigger out of instinct rather than choice. The gun went off with a roar.

Grandpa Eng grunted, but his momentum carried him forward so that he slammed into Eddy. Eddy's wig went flying into the air as the two of them went over.

Auntie was moving forward even as they fell.

"Wait," I shouted as I followed her.

Grandpa Eng was lying on top of the younger man. As Eddy struggled to toss him aside, Grandpa Eng whipped his arms around him and held on grimly.

Auntie snatched up the wrench from where it had fallen and raised it over her head as she ran. She brought it down hard on Eddy's wrist. Screaming, he dropped the gun.

The next moment I had grabbed his other arm and pinned it to the floor.

Auntie dropped the wrench and picked up the gun. In a movie Auntie could hold a gun steady and true, but they were always props with fake bullets. Now that she was holding the real thing, her hand shook dangerously. She was as likely to hit one of us as Eddy when she tried to aim it.

"Don't try anything," she warned.

"I'm not going to jail," Eddy said. He swung his head up so that his forehead hit Grandpa Eng's jaw hard. With a moan, Grandpa Eng went limp.

"I'll shoot," Auntie said, but the gun was shaking even more now.

Eddy must have been working out, or maybe it was fear of jail that gave him strength, because he threw Grandpa Eng off himself and into Auntie's legs. With a shout, Auntie toppled over again.

"Auntie," I said. As I hurried toward her, Eddy dashed past me on his way out.

"Stop," Chris said, jumping in his path.

Eddy tossed my brother aside as if he were a pillow.

"Take care of them," Chris said, getting his balance.

"Don't do anything stupid," I warned, suddenly worried. "Let the police handle it."

"That's my trouble. I've been standing by the sidelines watching everyone else do stuff. But you and Auntie actually get in the game and play it. I'm not letting that scum get away with this," Chris said, and he disappeared toward the stairs.

"But you'll get yourself killed," I shouted. I was surprised at how scared that made me. Why did he have to start acting like a hero now? All I'd wanted was a slightly mellower brother. Chris could be as cowardly as he wanted, as long as he stayed alive.

Auntie was sitting up, feeling Grandpa's pulse. "He's okay. It looks like just a flesh wound."

Grandpa's eyelids fluttered up. *"So I'm not dead?"* he croaked.

"You're going to get older, Grandpa Eng," I promised him as I took his hand.

"*I was afraid of that,*" he said, and he shut his eyes again.

"Chris went after Eddy," I said frantically.

"We'll get help," Auntie said, and she picked up the gun.

We ran around the machinery. I thought I might get lost, but somehow I managed to remember the way. Hurrying up the steps, our feet hit the treads pretty hard, making them groan. A couple of times I thought the boards were going to break.

At the top of the stairs, we heard thudding from the "courthouse." When we got to the doorway, we saw Chris and Eddy locked together, twisting in circles.

"Just let him go, Chris, you stupid jerk," I yelled frantically.

Unfortunately, that distracted Chris just enough. His head half turned toward me. By the time he caught himself, Eddy's head was moving forward again to butt Chris.

Chris tried to twist to the side, but Eddy's forehead caught his chin. As Chris staggered backward, Eddy whirled around to run.

I'd never seen Chris so determined before. As he fell, he whipped out a leg and caught Eddy's calf.

Eddy tumbled sideways, straight into the Judge's throne. As he dropped to his knees, the Judge of the Dead seemed to come to life, nodding his head as if he were coming to some decision.

"Watch out," Auntie shouted to Eddy.

I heard a crack as a faulty leg on the throne broke. I remembered how wobbly it had been when Clark had leaned against it.

With a cry Eddy tried to get to his feet as the Judge and his throne toppled forward. I didn't know how much the wax figure weighed, but the throne looked heavy enough as it smashed into Eddy.

Eddy had just been tried and sentenced for his sins by the Judge of the Dead.

"You can't escape the Judge," Auntie said quietly.

CHAPTER EIGHTEEN

Grandpa Eng's hospital room was crowded with people, though Clark had the only chair.

"So you may have cheated the Judge of the Dead by saving Eddy's life," Auntie said, rearranging the flowers she had brought. "But the Judge always gets his due—with the help of a human counterpart. Eddy should be going to prison for a long time." She had that on good authority, from Norm.

"Judge always win." Grandpa Eng nodded from his bed.

"I'm going to see Eddy next," Clark was saying. "He's under police guard in another wing. Just a slight concussion. I'll see to it that he has the best lawyer money can buy."

"But he tried to kill you," I said.

Clark looked embarrassed. "If I hadn't been such an insensitive jerk, maybe none of this would have happened. I'm the one who made poor Eddy explode like a firecracker."

So Eddy had been wrong. Clark was trying to change. Lucky for Eddy.

"It's a good thing Auntie was around," Chris said.

"Zing, zap." Clark snapped his fingers. "I told Manny that things happen when you're around. I bet we could get a whole season of stories just by talking to you for a couple of hours."

"Let's do it." Auntie nodded.

Grandpa Eng sipped some water. "Soon you even more famous than before," he said.

Auntie stepped back to study her work. "I'd have to go some to match you."

Taped to the wall behind the bed were the front pages of the newspaper. The headlines ranged from "Heroic Man Saves Film Star" to "Avenging Laundryman." The big photos all showed Grandpa with a magnificent black eye.

Grandpa Eng turned and pointed to the "laundryman" headline. "I not do much." The motion hurt his injured side and made him wince.

"What did I tell you about sitting still?" Evie asked in exasperation. She reached behind him to plump his pillow. She had adopted him as her grandfather, and she and Chris had spent almost every day here.

Judging from the goofy way my brother came home from the hospital every night, I supposed I was going to have to get used to her. Still, if I had to be locked up in a room with a ton of explosives, there could have been worse company than Evie.

Grandpa Eng nodded to Chris. "You the one catch him though. You should get headline."

171

"You faced down a loaded gun. I just finished what you started." Chris took the glass from Grandpa Eng's hand and filled it from a pitcher on the nightstand.

"You spoil me," Grandpa Eng said. "You all spoil me." He glanced at Clark. "Thank you for room."

"It's disgusting that you aren't even covered by a health plan," Clark said. "It's the least I can do for the man who kept me from blowing up."

"But I just fall," Grandpa Eng protested.

"But it was in the right direction," Auntie said, laughing.

"I bet your grandson was proud of you," I said.

From the sad expression on Grandpa Eng's face, I knew it was the wrong thing to say.

"He hasn't come by," Chris said.

"He'll come around," Auntie tried to assure him.

"I hope so," Grandpa Eng said.

I guess it was too much to hope that things would have a happy ending like in the movies.

"Without you, he'd never have gotten out," I said. "He ought to be grateful."

"No, he got out because all you." He waved a hand again to indicate everyone gathered in the room. Then he gripped Auntie's hand. "See. I know you fix things good."

"There's the man," Manny boomed from the doorway. With him was Marie, the girl from the sandwich shop.

"You've got to start pumping Tiger Lil for ideas too, Manny," Clark urged.

Auntie held her arm away from her side like the handle of a pump. "I'm primed and waiting."

Manny grinned. "I found something even hotter. Marie's right out of the headlines."

Marie was too much in awe of Clark to take a step, so Manny put his arm around her shoulders and drew her forward. "This little lady called, and it's our lucky day that I happened to answer the phone."

"I had Clark's number," Marie confessed. "It was just a fan call. Thank you so much, Tiger Lil."

Manny spread his arms excitedly. "Just wait until you hear how she escaped from the Communists in Vietnam. The things she had to do to come to America!"

"I thought we were going to take our story lines from Tiger Lil," Clark said.

"Sure, sure, and I still want to," Manny said quickly. "But maybe next season. You understand, don't you, Tiger Lil? You're a pro."

"I understand you, all right," Auntie said, sighing.

"Let's do Marie next season. I want to go with Tiger Lil's story line," Clark said stubbornly.

"It's okay, Clark," Auntie said. "Talk to me about next season."

"This is the way I see it. Marie's a street-wise punk," Manny said, beginning to gesture wildly with his arms. "You rescue her, but she falls in love with Warren. Zip. Zing. We got a triangle."

"What about Evie?" Chris demanded. I hoped he wasn't going to start throwing punches.

"What about her?" Manny asked. He seemed to have forgotten all about the earlier conversation about an audition.

"But—" Chris tried to protest.

Evie squeezed his hand. "Actually, Chris, after hanging around with your aunt on the set, I think there are easier ways of making a living."

From what I'd seen of her acting ability, maybe it was just as well.

"I've tested Marie," Manny said, and he looked at her proudly. "She's a natural."

Marie was looking a little overwhelmed. "It's all like a dream."

"I know talent," Manny declared. "I found Clark, didn't I?"

"I love movies," Marie gushed. "When I was little I'd go to the theater, and then I'd act them out when I'd go home."

"You see?" Manny said. "Just like I said. A natural."

"She's going to need a grandmother, though," Clark demanded.

Manny wiped his hand over an invisible chalkboard. "Zap that. Marie's got to be an orphan. No family at all."

"I won't do it without Tiger Lil," Clark said. He started to look stubborn.

"Sorry to end run you, but I've already pitched to the network and they love it," Manny said, and he made a sizzling sound. "They think it's just the juice the show needs. They're going to do all sorts of publicity. Warren likes it too. We're going to set up a love triangle."

Clark folded his arms. "I don't care, Manny. I'll go to the mat on this one."

Manny rubbed his head. "We'd hate to do it without you, but we will."

Clark swallowed in surprise, but he held firm. "I dare you to go ahead."

Auntie cleared her throat suddenly. "Actually, Clark, I meant to talk to you. I really think a grandmother part is too old for me."

I knew how much Auntie wanted to be in the show. I think she was doing it to save Clark. In fact, it might have been the bravest thing she had done so far.

"A friend then," Clark suggested. "Or maybe a landlady."

Manny started to get excited. "We'll make her your aunt. Put her in for six episodes and see how it goes."

Clark consulted Auntie. "Does that work for you, Tiger Lil?"

"Sure," Auntie said, hiding her disappointment.

As Clark and Manny discussed the new development, I whispered to Auntie, "That's not fair. If you hadn't given Marie the telephone number, she would never have talked to Manny. She was supposed to use that to phone for help, not make a fan call."

Auntie shrugged stoically. "That's show biz, kiddo."

At that moment someone tapped at the door. "Excuse me. May I come in?" Mr. Chan asked timidly.

"This is the man whose granddaughter I was telling you about," Auntie said to Clark.

"Yes, the food poisoner," Clark said.

Mr. Chan froze when he saw Clark. "Oh, my goodness," he mumbled several times. "I wish I had brought my granddaughter."

"I saw a doctor. I do have an ulcer, so we're not canceling the contract. No hard feelings, I hope." Clark was busy scribbling something on a card. "I understand from Tiger Lil that your granddaughter's my number-one fan. So have her call this number. The production company secretary can set up a time for us to chat one-on-one."

As he took the card, Mr. Chan began to mutter again, "Oh, my goodness." When he slipped it into his wallet, he treated it as if it were plated in gold.

Auntie cleared her throat. "And I think you know this gentleman," she said, indicating Grandpa Eng.

Mr. Chan smiled broadly as he held out his hand. "How are you doing?"

"Best bed I have for years," Grandpa Eng said, patting the bed.

"Well, I was wondering what you were going to do once you're out of here," Mr. Chan said.

Grandpa Eng shrugged. "I go back to laundry."

"My uncle says he'll hold the job for you," Evie said, "such as it is."

"He's made peace with your family?" Auntie asked her.

"No, but at least he's talking to me," Evie said. "And that's a big step. He really didn't recognize me before."

"Well, Mr. Eng, I wish you'd think about coming to work for me," Mr. Chan said. "I have all sorts of burglar alarms, but I still like to have someone in the building. I'd pay you, of course."

Grandpa Eng looked as if that were tempting, but he shook his head. "I too old. You need watchman."

Mr. Chan chuckled. "I already know how strong you are, but all you'll have to do is listen for anything suspicious and call the police if you hear something. There's a studio apartment in the back of the building. So you'd have to be there at night, but you'd be free during the daytime."

Grandpa Eng sat up excitedly. "I could go to Chinatown in daytime?"

"Wherever you want," Mr. Chan said. "I only need you at night."

"I could go to lunch. Treat my friends. That nice," Grandpa Eng said thoughtfully.

"Well, you think about it." Mr. Chan gave Grandpa Eng his card. "Just give me a call before you get out of the hospital."

"Thank you," Grandpa Eng said.

As Mr. Chan turned away from Grandpa Eng, he winked at Auntie. When he was gone, I plucked at Auntie's sleeve. "Did you have something to do with that?" I whispered.

"It would have occurred to Mr. Chan eventually," Auntie murmured. "I just helped speed up the process."

"Is there any mess that you can't resist fixing?" I asked.

Auntie grinned. "Nope."

We left a little after that, when Grandpa Eng wanted to nap. Chris and Evie went off to the cafeteria hand in hand. Clark, Manny, and Marie sat down in some chairs in the waiting room, scribbling down story ideas.

As we rode down in the elevator, I glanced at Auntie. "I'm sorry."

If I was expecting some self-pitying, sagging actor, I was wrong. Auntie was bouncing up and down on the balls of her feet. She turned to look at me quizzically. "Sorry for what, kiddo?"

I thought it weird that I had to explain. "They were going to do all those shows for you. Now Marie will be the star," I complained.

Auntie smiled at her reflection on the shiny elevator doors. "The more I think about it, the more I don't want to tie myself up in television for a long time." She made a minute adjustment to her hair.

I nudged her. "You're with me. You don't have to pretend anymore. You don't have to hide your disappointment."

Auntie laughed as she lowered her hands. "Carl's right. Television is too much like an assembly line. Six episodes will be about right. Movies are what any real actor wants. This way I'll get the exposure on Clark's show, but I'll be able to keep my options open for film projects. All those Hollywood producers will realize Tiger Lil's still alive and available."

I should have known. Auntie's heart was like a helium balloon. Its natural motion was always upward. If there was a storm, she'd always find the clear patch to sail through.

However, I was still upset for her. "But what will you do in the meantime?"

The doors opened, and Auntie strutted out into the lobby. "I got my kids to get jobs for, and my public relations biz for starters. And you saw what I did for Grandpa Eng, and I cleared Chris. In my spare time, I'll find what's broke and take care of it," she said.

"There's a lot in Chinatown that needs fixing," I agreed.

As the hospital's front doors automatically slid open for

us, Auntie hooked her arm through mine. "Maybe I'm a better fixer than an actor."

"You're both," I said as we stepped outside. "Chinatown's been a lot more fun since you got back."

Outside, the sun had finally broken through the clouds that had been lingering over the city for weeks. The warmth felt good on my face.

Auntie leaned her head against mine. "You know, kiddo, I'm going to have new cards made up, I think." She bent her fingers and moved her arm in a line. "Ms. Fix-It."

I laughed. "That's just what you need. Another title for your card."

She gazed absently up at the sunny sky as she began to design the card in her mind. Well, I supposed, finding the sunshine was her job.

"Auntie, watch out for the pothole," I said.

"Maybe in red and gold," Auntie murmured as I steered her around the hole.

I guessed that was my job.

Maybe I'd get some cards too.

LAURENCE YEP grew up in San Francisco, where he was born. He attended Marquette University, was graduated from the University of California at Santa Cruz, and received his Ph.D. from the State University of New York at Buffalo.

His many novels include *Dragonwings*, a Newbery Honor Book of 1976 and the recipient of the International Reading Association's 1976 Children's Book Award, and *Dragon's Gate*, a Newbery Honor Book of 1994. The author of many other books for children and young adults, he has also taught creative writing and Asian American studies at The University of California, Berkeley and Santa Barbara. In 1990 he received an NEA fellowship in fiction.